CW01081172

Knights in the Past
Book 3
A Queen Arthur Adventure

Published by: Crimson Myth Press
(www.CrimsonMyth.com)
Edited by: Lorelei Logsdon (www.LoreleiLogsdon.com)
Cover art: Amy P. Simmonds
(www.AmyPSimmonds.com)
Cover Text: Jake T. Logsdon (www.JakeLogsdon.com)

ACKNOWLEDGEMENTS

This one is dedicated to those who have a warped sense of humo(u)r!

Thanks to the *Knights in the Past* launch group!
(listed in alphabetical order by first name)

Adam Goldstein, Adam Pederick, Camille E. Green, Carolyn Jean Evans, Christopher Ridgway, Dan Sippel, Debbie Tily, Diann Pustay, Eden England-Woods, Fiona Sanders, Grant Taft Lewis, Helen Day, Ian Nick Tarry, Jackie Spencer, Jamie Smith, Jan Gray, Jodie Stackowiak, John Debnam, Karen Atkinson, Karen Brown, Lizzy Marjot, Lynette Wood, Mark Brown, Matthew Stuart Thomas Wilson, Michael Illingworth, Noah Sturdevant, Pamita Rao, Ray Sipe, Sandee Lloyd, Sharon Kennedy, Stephen Bagwell, Teresa Cattrall Ferguson, Ty Seale.

THE PAST IS PRESENT

ARTHUR, GUINEVERE, ARTY, Merlin, Galahad, Bors de Ganis, Kay, and Gaheris all stood in front of a couple of Roman guards who were wielding swords.

The landscape around them signaled that Merlin had been correct in his assumption regarding where they'd landed. This was definitely Ancient Rome. At least according to the descriptions Arthur had read when in school as a lad. There were large buildings in the distance with columns and grand architecture, the grounds were immaculately manicured, people wore little white outfits called "two goes" or something like that, and the guard uniforms were made of that dark leather that Arthur had always found to be fashionable.

While he was certain his knights could easily overpower the two men, especially since one was a bit old and somewhat portly and the other was so thin it was amazing he could hold the sword up at all, Arthur recognized this wasn't Camelot. That meant a skirmish with these two would likely result in bringing the full bore of the Roman guards down upon their heads.

But Sir Gaheris had already started making his trademarked "Gah" and "Guh" sounds that signaled he was readying for battle. And even if you missed the sounds, it wouldn't be long before you caught wind of his preparations.

"Calm yourself, Gaheris," Arthur commanded.

Gaheris grimaced. "But I'm already halfway prepared, sire. I can't easily stop now."

"Well, go over behind that boulder and do what you must."

Gaheris began to carefully pad off to the rock as Arthur shook his head at the man.

Guinevere sighed at Arthur in her way. This was a common thing with his beloved as Arthur seemed to always be doing the wrong thing in one fashion or another, at least in her eyes. But she was his radiant lady... even though she was currently wearing a green top that was cut like one belonging to a ranger and a pair of brown pantaloons that were unheard of for a lady to wear in royal circles. To be fair, though, Arthur had on a green gown and a fresh round of makeup that he'd put on when in Allison's restroom in the future.

"Where does he think he's going?" asked the thin guard, pointing his sword at the departing Gaheris.

"Oh, sorry," Arthur said, remembering their current predicament. "He's gone to relieve some pressure."

"You mean he's taking a—"

Arthur nodded. "Yes."

"I believe there's a fine for that," announced the portly man.

The two guards looked at each other for a moment and nodded.

To Arthur, this clearly indicated there wasn't likely a fine, which was a good thing since they didn't have any currency for this day and age. They hadn't had any in the future either, but they were able to get by using their ingenuity, along with Sir Lance-A-Lot's extra appendage, of course. Unfortunately, Lance wasn't here. Arthur cringed at the fact that he thought it unfortunate.

"What should we do, Arthur?" said Merlin, leaning in to whisper.

The little wizard—or was it "scientist" now?—had on his purple hat (the one covered in stars and moons), a matching jacket, a white shirt that represented some fellow who appeared to be dancing, and the words "Elvis Lives" stenciled on it, and a pair of pants he referred to as "jeans."

"You're the one who got us into this mess, Merlin," Arthur whispered back.

"Right, but you're the kingly sort." Merlin paused and glanced over Arthur in his current garb. "Well, queenly, I guess, but—"

"Oh, so *now* I'm a king?" Arthur said, his voice on the rise. "All those years I've attempted to treat you like one of my subjects and you did nothing but tell me how you didn't go in for that hoopla. But we face a bit of trouble and suddenly having royalty around is comforting, eh?"

"No, you dullard," replied Merlin, "it's because these two are guards from a different age. And while they will undoubtedly *not* know the name of Merlin, they should well see that flash of royalty that you carry about as if born with it!"

"Oh, right. Sorry." Arthur looked at his feet for a moment before realizing the full breadth of what Merlin had said. "Hey, wait, I *was* born with it."

"No, you achieved it upon finding *Excalibur*."

"Achieved," Arthur conceded, "but by birth it was my destiny."

Merlin waved his hand. "Semantics."

"Sorry to interrupt this engrossing dialog," said the thin guard, "but who exactly are you people?"

Arthur cleared his throat and stood up tall, puffing his chest out.

"I am King Arthur of Camelot."

The chubby guard leaned over. "What did he say?"

"I think he said he's the king of a lot of camels."

"No," said Arthur, furrowing his brow. "I said the King of Camelot."

"Is that where all the camels come from?" asked the heavy one.

"I..." Arthur began, but then blinked a few times. "What?"

Arty, the king of Scotland, who was wearing a leopard-skin outfit that was barely covered by the jacket he'd had on, pushed through and said, "Let me try, yeah?" He then turned to the guards. "Listen, ye couple of daft peons. I dinnae know what it is ye do in yer army of sorts, but we're after bein' a couple of kings, yeah?"

"You two are a couple, then?" asked the portly guard.

"What?"

"They are both wearing women's clothes," noted the thin one. Then he glanced back quickly. "Not that I'm judging you."

"Oh, no," agreed the portly one vehemently. "Definitely no judging going on over here. No sirree."

"Ah, that," Arty said as his eyes darted around. "Uh... We were at a costume party is all."

"Sure, sure," the thin guard said with a quick nod.

The fat one squinted. "Anyway, were you summoned by the emperor or something?"

"I dinnae think so," answered Arty.

"Yes!" Merlin yelped. "Yes, we were summoned by the emperor. Exactly that."

The portly guard reacted suspiciously to Merlin's outburst. He lowered his sword slightly, tapping a nearby rock with it. He gave a sideways glance to his partner before setting his eyes back on Merlin.

"What's his name, then?"

"Sorry?"

"The Emperor of Rome," replied the fat one. "What's his name?"

"Uh... Well, it's been a while since we got the invitation." Merlin swallowed and began chewing his lip. "Let's see..." He snapped his fingers. "Ah yes, Bulbus Headus."

"No."

"Flatulate?" offered Merlin.

"That's his brother," replied the fat one.

"*Was* his brother," corrected the thin one.

"Oh yes, true."

"Isn't it close enough that we know his brother's name?" asked Merlin.

The fat one shook his head. "Sure isn't."

"Pardon me," said Galahad, raising his hand. He wore his standard garb, which consisted of plate armor, chainmail, and a crimson tabard that housed the drawing of a lion. It was the exact same garb worn by all of the knights in their party. "What year is it?"

"You don't know what year it is?" said the thin one confusedly.

"We're from a different land than you," explained Galahad. "Our calendars aren't likely the same."

"Oh, that makes sense, I guess. Fine, it's what we call 72AD." The thin one looked up. "No idea what the AD stands for, though. Sorry."

Galahad nodded firmly and declared, "Vespasian

is your emperor."

"Nope."

"No?" Galahad replied, shocked. "But I was just reading a periodical on Roman history not two weeks ago—"

"You were?" interrupted Arthur.

"Yes, sire. I thought certain—"

"Vitellius?" announced Sir Gaheris, having come back from his mission on the other side of the boulder.

"Nope."

"Titus?" said Gaheris, scratching his head.

"Not even close."

"Too early for him yet, Sir Gaheris," stated Galahad, "but I'm impressed you know any of these names."

"My father was a history teacher."

Galahad gawked at that. "And he taught you?"

"I learned what I learned."

The thin guard waved his sword around menacingly. "What are you two going on about?"

"Yeah," agreed the portly one. "I'm about to stick my sword in one of you."

"Always sounds funny when you say that, Buttus Facius," the thin guard said with a giggle.

"Grow up, Thumpus Rumpus," retaliated Buttus Facius.

"Your names are Thumpus Rumpus and Buttus Facius?" said Bors de Ganis more loudly than he probably should have.

"Yeah, so?" said Thumpus.

"What of it?" agreed Buttus.

"Nothing," Bors replied, obviously refocusing on the swords in front of him. "Just clarifying, is all."

Just as Arthur was about to speak up again, Merlin reached over and grabbed his arm. The old man took a step forward until the points of the swords were touching his chest. Arthur was no wizard—or scientist, as the case may be—but he knew that pointy blades were quite adept at piercing flesh.

"You know," said Merlin as he clasped his hands behind his back studiously, "I'm starting to wonder why you're asking us for your emperor's name."

"For proof that you were invited," said Buttus.

"Could be," Merlin allowed, "or maybe it has something to do with the fact that you don't know his name yourselves and you're hoping we'll jog your memories."

"It's a conspiracy," Galahad said, obviously catching on to the ruse.

"That's not true," said Thumpus.

"Yeah, we know his name," agreed Buttus.

Merlin scoffed. "Sure you do."

"We do!"

"Most assuredly," Buttus again backed up his partner.

"Uh-huh." By now, Merlin was looking at his fingernails.

"Your lack of faith in our word is trying on my nerves," Thumpus said, his eye twitching.

Buttus grew dark. "And mine as well."

Merlin spun away dramatically, allowing his purple robe to float upward. He took two steps before spinning back and pointing at the guard known as Thumpus Rumpus.

"Prove it, then," demanded Merlin. "What's his name?"

"It's Emperor Flaccidus!"

"Technically," amended Buttus, "it used to be Emperor Longus Dongus, but he's gotten a bit older."

Thumpus calmed slightly. "True. And that bet he lost..." He trailed off and then set his stare back on Merlin. "So, there you go, we have proved to you that we do indeed know our emperor's name. What have you to say to that?"

"My apologies," Merlin answered with a bow. On his way back up he added, "Arthur?"

Without missing a beat, Arthur said, "We'd like to speak with Emperor Flaccidus immediately!"

"So you *do* know his name," Thumpus Rumpus said with a satisfied grin.

"All right, then," Buttus Facius said, replacing his sword in its scabbard, "follow us."

JUPITER

THE INSIDE OF the spaceship looked precisely like you'd expect the inside of a spaceship to look. It was covered in metallic tones, clean lines, video panels, and stations littered with flashing lights, blue buttons, and black knobs. What you wouldn't have expected was the nice living area with a large couch, shag carpeting, and a wide-screen television.

Jupiter and his current wife, Leto, were seated on said couch, watching their favorite show, *CSI: Alpha Centauri*.

Jupiter was a large man with stark gray hair that was styled in such a way to make him appear to always be running. His skin was tanned, which made little sense being that he was rarely ever out in direct sunlight, and his muscles bulged nearly as much as his belly. He *had* been getting old, after all.

Leto was far younger than Jupiter and she was a real beauty. Long, dark hair, emerald-green eyes, perky coconuts, and her skin was flawless. She looked as gorgeous now as she had the day Jupiter met her on their first date from a match on an intergalactic dating site.

The TV show was just about to the point where the big chase was going to happen. Jupiter loved this part of the show. It made his heart race. Plus, he always liked to guess who the culprit was, and so far he was right nearly eighty percent of the time.

"Yo, Dad," Apollo called from one of the terminals in his slightly feminine voice, "looks like something is going on here."

It happened every time.

"Your mother and I are watching a movie, Apollo."

"But—"

"There's fifteen minutes left, Apollo," Jupiter said more tightly.

"Yes, but—"

"Damn it," Jupiter yelled, pausing the video and throwing the remote across the room. "Why do you always do this, boy? You've never got anything to say until I'm right in the middle of something. If I'm watching TV, you interrupt me right before the best part; if I'm on the phone with one of my cousins, you're constantly nagging me to the point where I have to hang up; and let's not even get into what you do during the Olympics!"

"Sorry, Dad," Apollo replied sheepishly. "Just thought you'd want to know about this. It's, well, unexpected."

Apollo glared at the boy, unable to keep his eye from twitching. One look at Apollo told you that he came from the loins of Jupiter. Same hair, though darker; same build, though without the belly; same eyes, though without the crow's feet; and same ability to allure the ladies, though Apollo preferred the gents.

"Calm yourself, Zeus," Leto said, patting her husband's arm lovingly.

"You know you shouldn't use that name, Leto." Jupiter pushed off the couch and went to retrieve the remote, hoping he hadn't broken it again. "Seriously, how many times do I have to ask you to call me Jupiter?"

"What difference does it make?"

"We're all about the Romans right now, so we have to stick with the program. When we refocus on the Greeks, you can go back to calling me Zeus."

Sure enough, the remote was broken. That was the third one this month. Fortunately he kept a supply of them in the drawer under the television.

"It's all such a pain," complained Leto. "We're the gods, right? Why should we have to change our names to suit them?"

Jupiter dug out a new controller and started putting batteries into it.

"It's easier for us to gain acceptance that way. Just roll with it, okay?"

"If you say so."

"Okay, son," Jupiter said, after snapping the back on the remote, "what's so damned important this time?"

"Forget it," replied Apollo while crossing his arms.

"Oh no, I'm not forgetting it." Jupiter took to wagging his finger. "You interrupted me with something spaceship-shattering in your estimation, so what is it?"

Apollo rolled his eyes and uncrossed his arms. "Fine. It looks like King Arthur from England, King Arthur from Scotland, Guinevere, Merlin, and a number of the Knights of the Round Table have just appeared near one of the walls by Emperor Flaccidus's royal palace."

"What?" said Jupiter, dropping the remote.

Athena, who was sitting in a nearby chair reading a Yogsdon and Lung novel, sat up and said, "Is Lance-A-Lot with them?"

"No," Apollo replied sadly.

Athena frowned and stuck her head back into her reading.

Jupiter had always considered Athena to be his most beautiful daughter. Dark hair, emerald eyes, and that same tanned tone that Jupiter was ingrained with. But she had a sinister streak that made up for that beauty. Of course, most of the gods did.

"Why do you ask that?" said Jupiter and he reached in for another remote.

"No reason," answered Athena.

"No reason, indeed," Leto said with a knowing smirk.

"Sounds to me like there's a reason." Jupiter quickly moved to put the remote in a safe place. "What are you two ladies talking about?"

"Oh, it's nothing, dear," Leto. "She's obviously heard tales from that *other* daughter of yours."

"Are you referring to Aphrodite again?" said Jupiter with a raised eyebrow. "Whenever you say *other daughter* like that you're always talking about her."

"If we're keeping with the Greek naming convention, yes."

"If I've told you once, I've told you a million times: She's not mine!"

Leto sniffed. "So you say."

"Okay, here we go again," said Jupiter, who was now pacing in front of the television. "When Cronus castrated Uranus and dumped the parts in the sea, Venus—or Aphrodite, in this case—arose from the sea foam on a giant scallop and walked to the shore in Cyprus."

"Riiiiiight," said Leto with a load of sarcasm lacing her voice, "and, if I recall correctly, Athena here came from your forehead."

"Hey," said Athena, "don't drag me into this."

"That's exactly what happened with Athena," said Jupiter, feeling his ire rising. "I told you already that it all started when I was going to bang Metis, but I felt bad about—"

"Getting caught," Leto interrupted.

Jupiter paused. "What? No! I felt that it was *wrong*. But it was kind of late by then and so I had to swallow her."

"Shouldn't that have been the other way around?" said Apollo.

Athena thought to throw her book at him, but deemed it far too valuable. Instead, she merely said, "Gross."

"Honestly, Zeus," Leto said, standing up and heading for the kitchen.

"It's Jupiter," Jupiter corrected, hot on her heels. "Anyway, as I've told you many times, it turned out that Metis was already preggers."

"And how do you suppose that happened?" Leto said over her shoulder.

"Uh..." Jupiter cursed to himself, but pressed on. "Well, anyway, I swallowed her up, you know? Then my stomach starts to hurt and I got the meanest headache you can imagine. Boy, let me tell you, that was one nasty motherf—"

"Forget about it, Zeus," Leto said, pushing past him and back to the main room while carrying a glass of wine.

"Again, it's Jupiter." He waited for her to sit back down. "Anyway, the next thing I know, she just popped out of my forehead. It was pretty surreal."

Leto took a sip of the wine and swirled the remainder in the glass. "I'm never going to buy these silly stories, Jupiter."

"It's Jupiter!" He blinked a couple of times. "Oh, you said that. Sorry. Anyway, it's true, I tell you. It's all true."

"Sure it is, dear."

"It is, and if you think normal childbirth is painful, try having a full-grown adult—who is wielding an axe, by the way—leap out of your forehead."

Leto took another sip after saying, "Ridiculous."

"It truly was," Jupiter replied, accepting her meaning as *he'd* preferred.

Everything got quiet for a few moments. This was a rarity on the ship, and it usually followed one of these little spats. Jupiter was well aware that he was going to be in the proverbial doghouse yet again, which would have been avoided if only he'd be allowed to watch one of his damned shows in peace.

"What's going on?" said Pluto as he walked into the room.

Jupiter held back a groan. It was bad enough having to live on this tiny ship with Athena and Apollo, but at least they were his children... sort of. Pluto, however, was his brother. In fact, if the two men stood side by side, you'd have a hell of a time telling them apart, aside from the fact that Pluto kept his hair longer and tinted brown. Jupiter grunted. It wasn't that Pluto was a bad guy or anything, at least assuming you were a fellow god, but he had become a bit of a mooch over the last year. The deal was that he was going to stay on the ship for a couple of weeks while he searched for a ship of his own, but weeks turned into months, and now he was just another irritant who consumed a lot of food, fought for the remote, and played loud music in the middle of the normal sleep cycle.

"I was just explaining how Aphrodite is *not* my daughter," answered Jupiter.

"Ah, the old 'giant clam' story, eh?" Pluto said, opening a beer.

"Scallop," corrected Jupiter.

"What?"

"It was a giant scallop, not a clam."

Pluto looked at him. "What's the difference?"

"Mostly how they swim," Jupiter answered with a shrug.

"Oh yeah, that's right." He laughed to himself. "That story is a classic. Almost as good as the one about Athena here coming from your brain."

"It was my forehead, and—"

"Don't go there, Pluto," warned Leto. "It's not worth the effort."

"I'll take your word for it," said Pluto as he lumbered over toward Apollo's station. "Well, what's on the video screen that's so interesting?"

"It looks like—" started Apollo.

"King Arthur and some of his cohorts have arrived in Rome," answered Jupiter, interrupting his son.

"No shit?" said Pluto. "How did they go back in

time?"

"Not a clue," said Jupiter, "but I think I shall send Apollo and Athena to go and find out. "

"Really?" Apollo said excitedly.

"I see no other way to peacefully watch the end of this show."

"Sweet."

Athena bolted up and ran down the hall, saying, "I'll go get dressed!"

JUST NOT THE SAME

EMPEROR FLACCIDUS WAS lying on the comfortable lounge bench with his head propped upon the lap of his wife, Queen Slutius. She was feeding him grapes as he gazed up at her olive skin, large brown eyes, and fluffy lips. Seeing her beauty, though, only depressed him further.

"You seem unhappy again, my love," she said in a voice that the birds of the Tiber river swooned over. "Is it something you'd like to discuss?"

"Same problem as ever, I'm afraid," he said, glancing away as another grape touched his lips.

"Ah."

He rolled up to a seated position, looking at his age-weathered hands. He knew he wasn't the man he once was, but he had assumed there were at least another five or ten years of vigor remaining in his blood.

"We never have relations anymore," he said

irritably.

"I do."

Flaccidus glanced at her sharply. "What?"

"Uh..." she said with a cough. "*Sure* we do."

"Oh, right." Flaccidus stood and walked to one of the windows. "Well, not as often as we once did. We do it once a month, if I'm lucky."

"That's by your choice, my love."

"I know, I know. I'm not blaming you. It's just—"

"Dear," Slutius said, rising to walk over to his side, "this all happened when you hit the age of fifty and lost that bet with your brother at your birthday party."

"Don't remind me," he groaned.

The queen scratched the wall next to them. "I still can't believe you had him killed."

"I had no choice."

"You could have refused to follow through on the bet," she argued gently.

"And be seen as a man who doesn't uphold his obligations?" He crossed his arms at that. "Never!"

"Then why kill him?"

"Because *he* could have forgiven me the debt instead of... well... what he did."

"But to die over a name change?" Slutius chastised. "That seems rather petty, even for an emperor."

Flaccidus sniffed and moved his hands to his hips. Nobody understood the plight of a man except for another man. Just as women always stated—

rightfully—that childbirth is something a man could never comprehend, the same went for the challenges and competition of manhood.

"Do you have any idea how difficult it's been to go from a manly name like Longus Dongus to a wimpy name like Flaccidus?" he said desperately.

"No, but I do know that it's been ever since then that we've stopped having decent relations."

"Precisely my point," spat Flaccidus. "Brother or not, the man needed to die for doing that to me."

"But he was so good in the sack," she moaned as Flaccidus turned away.

He paused. "What was that?"

"Uh... You didn't have to break his back," Slutius replied hurriedly. "Horrible way to go."

"I poisoned him," said Flaccidus with a frown.

"Oh, that's right. Sorry."

Just as the emperor was about to question his wife further on the subject, there came a knock on the door. It was a rarity to be left alone for very long when running an empire.

"Enter," he called out, returning to the bench and seating himself.

Two of his guards walked in and knelt reverently before him. They were his most trusted men.

Hemorrhoidoclese stood a full head over the emperor and was built like a tank. Were he not so valued as a guard, Flaccidus would have loved to see him fight in the open battles. Next to him stood Suppositorius. Where he wasn't quite the physical specimen that Hemorrhoidoclese was, he was quick with the blade and firm of mind. When these two were around, Flaccidus felt safer... assuming there were no gods in the vicinity, of course.

"Yes?"

"Sorry to interrupt, my lord," rumbled Hemorrhoidoclese, "but some emissaries from a distant land claim to have been invited to visit you."

Flaccidus thought over his schedule. As far as he remembered, there were no planned visitations for at least another week.

"Who are they?" he asked.

"There are a couple of queens," began Suppositorius, "a king—"

"It's the other way around, Suppositorius," corrected Hemorrhoidoclese.

"Huh?"

"There are two kings, a queen, and a bunch of soldiers."

"Oh, yeah, that's right. Thanks, Hemorrhoidoclese."

"You bet."

Suppositorius turned back to Flaccidus, "Also, sire, there's an old guy with a pointy hat and strange clothing."

"Well, they're all wearing weird clothes," noted Hemorrhoidoclese.

"Especially the 'kings,'" said Suppositorius with a grin.

Hemorrhoidoclese smiled. "Haha... Yeah."

Flaccidus was not one who enjoyed being left in the dark. He cleared his throat expectantly.

"Sorry, sire," said Suppositorius, coming back to attention.

"Why did you use air quotes when describing the kings?" asked Flaccidus after a moment.

"You see, sire," said Hemorrhoidoclese, "it's that they're kind of dressed like, well—"

"Women," finished Suppositorius.

Hemorrhoidoclese pointed at his fellow guard and said, "Right."

"Oh?" said Flaccidus, finding that curious. "Well, send them in."

YER GOIN'

FAR OUTSIDE THE walls of Camelot, Ceallach stood at the edge of the camp where King Arthur of Scotland left him and the rest of the men a number of days before. It had been too long since his king had entered the English walls and Ceallach was finding himself on edge.

To that end, he had picked one of the men and told him to go into town and see what he could learn about their king's whereabouts.

"Are ye sure yer not wantin' to go yerself?" said a worried-looking soldier by the name of Doonan.

The two men stood side by side, staring out at Camelot. It looked majestic as the morning sun shone upon its walls. No better than their own castle back home, of course, but Ceallach had to admit that the banners hanging down the sides of the parapets were a nice touch.

He glanced at Doonan. The man had reddish hair

and a scraggly beard that would mark almost all the men at camp, but Doonan was one of the smallest in the entire Scottish Army. Ceallach knew better than to judge the fighting prowess of a person by size alone. He'd lost many a scuffle while clinging to that prejudice, in fact. But when it came to Doonan, one couldn't help but think the man was better suited to life outside the military.

Ceallach sighed and looked around at the others in camp. Any one of them would be better suited for the task at hand, but Doonan was what you might call "expendable."

"Ye'll be fine," answered Ceallach. "What can they do?"

Doonan gulped. "String me up by me nethers."

"Aye, true. Not likely, though. Our king says he's become friends with the English."

"Then maybe they're just after bein' in a party?" Doonan said hopefully. "Wouldn't want to bother him in that case, yeah?"

"Nay," Ceallach replied, staring off at Camelot. "The king said he'd be back. He's not after bein' back."

"Then maybe they've strung *him* up by *his* nethers," Doonan whispered.

"Hope not, but that's what you'll need to go find out."

"Calle, it's just—"

"Doonan," Ceallach said, turning on the smaller man and giving him a look that spelled doom, "yer goin' and I dinnae wanna here another word on it."

"All right, all right," Doonan said, backing away. "No point in gettin' yer kilt in a bunch." Then, as if trying to find solid footing again, he sternly said, "Just know this, Ceallach: I'm not layin' down me sword for no man."

"Ah, that reminds me," Ceallach said, pointing at Doonan's weapon, "leave yer sword behind."

Doonan's eyebrows jumped. "Didn't ye just hear what I said?"

"Ye still have yer axe," said Ceallach. "Now get on with ye!"

THE AUDIENCE

ARTHUR WAS IMPRESSED with the palace. The grounds were immaculately kept, the buildings were enormous and beautifully designed, especially all the columns and craftsmanship, and the use of marble was inspired. There were sculptures of people he couldn't have known, but they were made with such care he assumed they were either gods or past rulers.

Everyone else in his party seemed to be just as taken aback by the wonders they were seeing. Even Sir Gaheris appeared awed by the sights.

"Okay," Arthur said, bringing their attention back to the problem at hand, "when we go in there, let me do the talking."

"Why you?" asked Arty.

"Because I'm the king, that's why."

Arty puffed out his chest. "So am I."

"Yes, I know," conceded Arthur, "but none of your men are here, which means that I'm in a better position to claim kingship than you are."

"What the shet kind of logic is that? A king is a king no matter how many subjects he's after havin'!"

Arthur took a deep breath. "Let me put it this way: Who remains king when one kingdom falls to another kingdom?"

"The one who wins, ye daft Englishman!"

"And how many soldiers do you currently have to stand against mine?"

"Oh." Arty pursed his lips and looked at his feet. "Well, when ye put it that way."

"Harsh," noted Merlin.

The doors opened and a large guard waved them in.

"You may enter."

As if the outer area wasn't amazing enough, Arthur's jaw nearly dropped at the designs contained in this room. He knew it was the room of their emperor, but it was far superior to what Arthur had in his own day. He made a mental note to have a word or two with his designers if they ever got back safely.

In front of them sat an older man who was wearing a white outfit and a thin gold crown. He didn't exactly look kingly, especially with his thinning hair, rounded stomach, and hairy arms, but seeing that the guards were giving him proper respect, Arthur knew the man was indeed their ruler.

"Who is in charge here?" the emperor said.

Merlin spoke up first. "I thought you were."

"Merlin," hissed Arthur.

"Merlin is in charge?" the emperor said.

"No," replied the wizard, "*you* are in charge. It's your kingdom, right?"

Flaccidus stuck his tongue in his teeth and then made a popping sound with his lips. He cracked his neck from side to side as if trying to relax himself.

"I repeat," he said with a glare. "Who is in charge here?"

"Maybe he wants to play that 'Guess his name' game?" suggested Galahad.

"Ah, yes," agreed Merlin. "Good thinking, Galahad." The wizard cleared his throat and winked at the emperor, saying in a grandiose voice, "Emperor Flaccid Dong is in charge."

"Merlin, quiet," Arthur hissed again.

"It's not Emperor Flaccid Dong, you geriatric peasant," the emperor said hotly. "It's Emperor Flaccidus."

"Oh, that's right," Merlin said, deflated. "My apologies."

"Now, what I want to know is who in *your* group is in charge of *your* group?"

Arthur stepped forward. "That would be me. I am Arthur, King of Camelot."

"You're the king of the camels?" said Flaccidus while scrunching up his face.

"No, I'm the king of Camelot."

"Right, I heard you the first time." Flaccidus tilted his head to the side. "So there are a lot of camels in your kingdom, yes?"

"No, it's just the name of the place." Arthur was beginning to wonder how simple these people truly were. "There are no camels. Lots of horses, but no camels."

"Then why not call it Horsealot?" asked the emperor.

"It has nothing to do with the animals," Arthur said, fighting to keep his cool.

"Obviously a stupid kingdom," Flaccidus said flippantly.

Arthur felt the slap of that insult. "Excuse me?"

"Good thing there weren't a lot of ducks in their kingdom," joked the large guard.

"Well played, Guard Hemorrhoidoclese," said Flaccidus with a chuckle.

"What about those small, stubborn horses?" the smaller guard asked his companion.

Hemorrhoidoclese looked about thoughtfully and then snapped his fingers. "You mean the ass, Suppositorius?"

"Haha!" cried Flaccidus. "Assalot!"

"Ah! Good one." Hemorrhoidoclese laughed and then said, "How about the rooster... You know, cock?"

"One of my favorites," said Slutius from behind the emperor.

"Haha..." Flaccidus started and then quickly looked at the queen. "What?"

"Hmmm?" she replied innocently. "Just love how

they wake us up in the morning."

"There's the dik-dik," noted Suppositorius.

"Never heard of it," said the larger guard.

"It's a form of antelope."

"Dik-dikalot," Flaccidus said while laughing almost uncontrollably.

"Wouldn't mind visiting there," said Slutius with a dreamy sigh.

Flaccidus's laughter ceased instantly as he frowned at Slutius. She glanced away, looking uncomfortable.

"Enough of this," Flaccidus stated while returning his study to Arthur. "So you're a king, eh?"

"Yes."

"More of a queen—" started Suppositorius.

"Silence," Flaccidus said, quieting his guard. Then the emperor said over his shoulder, "Do kings have more power than emperors?"

"I don't believe so," replied Slutius. "Certainly not in your palace, anyway."

Flaccidus nodded at this. "So King Arthur, is it?"

"It is," Arthur replied proudly.

The emperor plucked a grape from the vine that was in the bowl next to him and popped it into his mouth. He chewed for a few moments as if thinking about what to say next.

"I've been told that I invited you to my palace."

"Right, about that—"

"Yet I don't recall inviting anyone to my palace by the name of Arthur."

"Yes, well, you see—"

"And yet you claim that I did."

"That's because—"

Flaccidus slammed his hands on the bench. "Explain yourself, man!"

"I've been trying to," Arthur replied angrily.

"No," countered Flaccidus, "you've been talking over me, and that's rude. When someone is speaking you should remain silent, dutifully listening along the way, and then speak when it is your turn."

Arthur softened. "My apologies. You are absolutely correct. In fact, I have actually had this very conversation with a couple of my own men a number of times."

"Accepted," Flaccidus said with a slow blink. "Now, explain why you lied to my guards."

"Because there was no other way to gain an audience with you," explained Arthur.

Flaccidus stuck another grape in his mouth. "And why do you require an audience?"

"Because we've traveled back in ti—"

"We're lost," Merlin interrupted, smacking Arthur on the arm.

"Ouch. What did you strike me for?" Arthur rubbed his bicep. "That hurt, you know?"

Merlin whispered, "You can't tell him we came back in time, you imbecile."

"Oh, right. Sorry."

Flaccidus stood up and approached them, studying their outfits. Arthur wasn't used to being placed under scrutiny as such, but he remained stoic, as did the others.

"Why are you all dressed so curiously?" Flaccidus asked, staring at the pointy hat on Merlin's head.

"Costume party," Guinevere said quickly. "We went to a costume party."

Flaccidus spun back to Slutius. "There was a costume party?"

"First I've heard of it," she answered.

"Guard Suppositorius, did you hear of a costume party?"

"No, my emperor."

"Nor did I, my liege," Hemorrhoidoclese answered before being asked.

"I see." He spun back to Guinevere. "Who threw this party?"

"You wouldn't know her."

"Try me."

"Okay," she said and then paused for a moment. "Uh, it was... Uh... Allison Smith. Yes, that's it. Allison Smith threw the party."

"Strange name," said Flaccidus as he walked away from them while rubbing his chin thoughtfully.

"What are you doing?" whispered Merlin as he leaned in front of Arthur to speak to Guinevere.

"Hopefully getting us out of trouble," Guinevere replied.

"But you shouldn't use her name."

"How can it hurt?"

Merlin opened his mouth a couple of times before saying, "Valid point."

"Guards," Flaccidus commanded a moment later, "I want this Allison Smith found and brought to me immediately."

"Of course, sire," said Hemorrhoidoclese, snapping his fingers at a few other soldiers who ran out of the room as if on a mission.

"Now, Arthur," Flaccidus said, "who are all these people with you?"

"This is my queen, Guinevere," Arthur replied. "That is Merlin, our uh... Court Jester."

"What?" said Merlin.

"This is King Arthur from Scotland."

"Wait," Flaccidus said, holding up a hand. "There are two kings with the same name?"

"I was as surprised as you," Arthur replied.

Flaccidus shrugged. "Okay, go on."

"The rest of these men are my knights. This is Sirs Kay, Bors De Ganis, Galahad, and Gaheris."

Flaccidus turned his gaze on the knights. To their credit, they remained firmly at attention while being inspected. This was most surprising of Gaheris, but Arthur assumed he was more relaxed since that visit to the boulder.

"You called these men 'nights.' Why is that? Do they only run about in the dark? Maybe they're on different shifts? Do you also have a group you call Dayts?" He looked outside. "No, that can't be it... It's still light out there."

"It's because..." Arthur trailed off. "Actually, I don't know. They're essentially elite soldiers, but I don't know where the term originated. Merlin?"

"Not a clue."

"Galahad?"

"I've never thought to look it up, to be honest, sire."

"Gaheris?"

"What?" said the gruff knight.

"You said your father was a history teacher, right?" asked Arthur.

"Yes, my lord."

"Well, do you have any idea where the term 'knight' originated?"

Gaheris looked uncomfortable, but said, "Depends on who you ask. My old dad never made clear, but he said that the accepted etymology comes from the Old English 'cnight.' That means 'boy' or 'servant.' But he'd also claimed there were other scholars who attributed it to the cognate of the Germanic 'knecht,' which is 'servant' or 'bondsman.'"

Bors gave Kay a surprised stare and said, "Is this honestly the same man who soils himself in public?"

"It's truly baffling," replied Kay in awe.

"Enough," demanded Flaccidus. Then he walked back to Arthur. "So these men are your boy-servants, then?"

"Excuse me?" said Bors.

"That's insulting," chimed Kay.

"Rather makes sense with that outfit you're wearing, Arthur," Flaccidus continued, clearly ignoring the knights.

"What?" Arthur said, looking down at himself. "No, it's—"

"A costume party. Yes, I'm aware." Flaccidus walked back to his bench and sat back down. "Now, King Arthur, tell me: Where precisely is your kingdom?"

"You may not want to say—" started Merlin.

"Britain," Arthur answered proudly.

"Oh boy."

"Is that so?" Flaccidus said with a twinkle in his eye.

"It is," replied Arthur. "Is that of particular interest?"

"Oh, indeed," answered the emperor.

"Why?"

"We've just always had problems with your country. But if you are the actual king, than I'd go as far as to say our problems are solved."

Arthur squinted. "Sorry, but how so?"

"Simple, you fool," Flaccidus said with a laugh. "If I execute you, your beloved Britain will no longer have a king!"

"I shall not stand for this," claimed Bors in a strong voice.

"Sit, then," suggested Flaccidus.

That seemed to confuse Bors. "Hmmm?"

"We'll block your every attempt, to protect our king," announced Kay, stepping forward strongly.

Flaccidus snapped up another grape casually and

began to chew it.

"I can have one hundred guards brandishing swords with the snap of my fingers," he stated flatly.

"Me too," Slutius said.

Flaccidus reeled around. "What's that?"

"Uh..." Slutius said, clearly catching herself, "I was just saying that it's true you could have guards in here quickly."

"Right," Flaccidus said at length.

And that's when Arthur heard the telltale sound that marked Sir Gaheris's plan to begin battling.

"Gah, guh."

Apparently his trip to the boulder hadn't been sufficient enough.

"What's that man doing?" Flaccidus said, pointing. Then he sniffed the air with a cringe. "And what is that infernal smell?"

Arthur dropped his shoulders. "You don't want to know."

"Is he soiling himself?"

"Yes."

"That's disgusting."

"Yes."

"Take them to the dungeon," commanded Flaccidus. "Quickly!"

THE DATA

LANCE-A-LOT was seated on the recliner, watching a spirited bout between two men in an octagonal cage. They were punching, kicking, twisting, and doing their best to bloody up each other. It was making him itch for battle.

That's when he smelled something that reminded him of Sir Gaheris.

His son, Mitch Jr., was making goo-goo noises on his lap, seeming rather pleased with himself. Lance picked up the boy to see if the smell was resonating from him. Sure enough, it was.

"I believe the boy has made another gift," Lance said to Allison.

"'Present,'" she corrected while keeping her face locked to the computer screen she'd been studying.

"Yes," said Lance, confused. "I'm here."

"No, I'm not asking you if you're present," she said, looking over her glasses. "I'm saying that the common vernacular for when a child fills its diaper is that they made a 'present,' not a 'gift.'"

"Ah, yes."

"So change him," she said as if it were nothing.

Lance-A-Lot had been through many challenges in his life. He'd fought down ruffians, saved maidens, laid maidens—often the very same ones he'd previously saved, been stabbed twice—once due to the jealousy of an angry husband over laying a self-proclaimed maiden that he'd previously saved, and even catered a party for fifty aristocrats. He was quite the chef, after all.

But never had he faced the horrors of diaper-changing.

"Uhhh..." he said worriedly.

Allison sighed and crossed her arms. Lance-A-Lot always felt worried when she did that because it meant he'd either done something wrong, was *doing* something wrong, or was *about* to do something wrong.

"Mitch," she said, using his actual name, "you can't just sit around watching sports and soap operas on television all day. You have to pull your own weight around here."

"Done that twice today already," Lance replied proudly.

"I don't mean it like that," she said with a frown. "I mean that you have to do your fair share of the work."

"Oh, right. Sorry, dear."

"Now, you change the boy while I go over some data."

It wasn't a request and so Lance set about to his task. He'd seen both Allison and Mrs. Smith, his new mother-in-law, change the boy on many occasions, so he knew the ins and outs of it. But there was something entirely different between watching such an event and participating in one.

In order to keep his mind off what he was doing, he said, "What is data, dear?"

"You don't know what data is?"

"Well, I know what it means, sure, but I only understand its use when dealing with the knights. They give me reports and I figure things out from it."

"Same thing, just that my reports come from the computer."

"Uh-huh," he said. She never gave him much information.

Allison must have recognized that she wasn't being very forthcoming, because she said, "Okay, I'll give you an example. When we sent Arthur and everyone back in time, the system logged information on it. That's data I can use to look at the efficiency of how many systems are running. From that I can derive if there are any needs for updates, performance enhancements, and so on." She began typing away on her keyboard. "So, I can pull up the information on their transport and..." She paused. "Huh."

"Something the matter?" asked Lance as he tried to keep himself from gagging.

"It's just that something looks…" Allison paused again. "Oh, shit."

"You can say that again."

"I sent them to the wrong time," she whispered.

"You mean like night or something?" said Lance as he powdered the boy's bottom.

"No, I mean like…" She began typing and clicking. "Oh boy. They're in 72AD."

Lance finished changing Mitch, Jr. and smiled at his handiwork. While it hadn't been pleasant, he was proud he'd accomplished something. Actually, the last time he'd felt this good about himself since moving in with Allison was when he'd successfully loaded the dishwasher.

He picked up Mitch, Jr., holding him for Allison to check out the accomplishment, but she was busily carrying a look of dread. That's when Lance replayed her last sentence over in his head.

"Are you saying that my king is in trouble?" he asked, feeling his body temperature instantly rise.

"I don't know," she replied, "but considering *where* they ended up, I'd say there's a strong possibility they are."

"What do you mean?"

"Well, they didn't just go back in time, they also landed in Ancient Rome."

Lance's eyes went wide. "What?"

TURKEY LEG

DOONAN WALKED UP the path that opened into Camelot. It didn't look all that different to him than his home kingdom, except for the litany of merchant carts lining the streets and pushing their wares. There were large ones, small ones, colorful ones, and plain ones. Some had wheels and some were clearly built for permanency.

He kept his head down, not wanting to engage anyone just yet. With any luck, he'd spot a soldier who would be able to help him find the king.

"You there," called out a merchant as Doonan stepped in a puddle, soaking his foot.

Doonan stopped and looked up at the merchant. It was a middle-aged man with a round face and beady eyes. He was standing behind a cart that had pieces of meat dangling from wires, and he was holding up a gigantic turkey leg.

Feeling rather self-conscious, Doonan pointed to

himself questioningly.

"Yes, you in the skirt," said the man. "Come over here and try a delightful turkey leg."

"It's a kilt," said Doonan, stepping over.

"No," replied the merchant, looking at the haunch of meat, "it's a turkey leg."

"I mean me skirt," explained Doonan. "It's called a kilt."

"Ah, well, glad that's cleared up." The merchant began wrapping up the foodstuff with a batch of brown paper. "Now, that will be three silver pieces for the turkey leg."

"I'm not after wantin' any turkey leg," Doonan said with a grimace. "I'm here on a mission to find me king."

"But you said you wanted the leg and I've gone and wrapped it."

"I've said no such thing, ya batty cart-pusher!"

A large man approached them. He was wearing a soldier's outfit that seemed similar to the one Doonan had seen the knights wearing when the king of England had visited a while back. But something didn't quite fit. This fellow had the look of a man who hadn't slept in many days, and the stench of alcohol that permeated from his being masked the merchant's delicacies in an instant.

"Okay, okay," said the man in a tired voice. "What's going on here?"

"Who're you?" asked Doonan.

"I am Sir Bedivere, a Knight of the Round Table."

"Truly?" Doonan said, appraising him once more.

"Yeah, why?"

"Ye just look like yer after bein' a fella that failed at sleepin' off a hangover."

"Well, that's about right," Bedivere replied with a nod, "but it's too early to start drinking again just yet. Now, what's going on here?"

"This man said he wanted a turkey leg and so I wrapped it up and now he won't pay," claimed the merchant.

"I dinnae want any damn turkey leg," Doonan argued. "Who's after eatin' somethin' like that this early in the morn?"

Bedivere glanced over at the merchant. "He's got you there."

"You're siding with him?" the merchant shrieked. "I'm a tax-paying citizen of this town. I pay your wage, man! This skirt-wearing fool is obviously an out-of-towner."

"Which means he's a tourist," Bedivere said pedantically. "The king always says that we could use more tourists to raise up our income."

"By selling turkey legs, I bring in money for the kingdom," the merchant was quick to note.

"Not if there aren't any tourists to buy your food," countered Bedivere.

"Bah," said the merchant. "Other people buy it all the time. I don't need any stinking tourists to pay me for turkey legs."

"I guess that makes the matter settled, then,"

Bedivere said with a satisfied smile.

"Damn," said the merchant, unwrapping the turkey leg and putting it back with the others. "I'm going to complain about this, I will."

"You do that," acknowledged Bedivere as he motioned Doonan to walk with him down the path. As soon as they were away from the grumbling shouts of the disgruntled merchant, Bedivere said, "You're from Scotland, yes?"

"How'd ye know?"

"Aside from the accent, you mean?"

"I have an accent?"

"It was your skirt that originally tipped me off."

"Kilt."

"Ah, right. Sorry." Bedivere rubbed his temples. "As you said, I'm still trying to clear my head from last night's boozing. Why are you here?"

Doonan felt that this man may prove helpful to his cause. He *had* been searching for a soldier, after all, and while this one appeared to be on the wrong-end of a beating, he also seemed decent enough.

"Looking for me king," said Doonan.

"Arthur?"

"It's a good sign that you're after knowin' his name."

"Named the same as ours," said Bedivere. "Hard to forget."

"Oh, aye. Seen him, then?"

"I haven't," admitted Bedivere, "but I recall two of the other knights saying that he was up in the wizard's lair, so chances are he's still there."

"Where's that after bein'?"

"It's up there," said Bedivere, pointing up the path. "I'll take you."

CHECKING IT OUT

APOLLO LANDED THE shuttle in its normal spot, just outside of town. The platform the Romans built as the landing site had the standard sculptures all around, but it was otherwise unadorned and flat. The view was barren except for straight ahead where the heart of the Roman Empire lay. Even at this distance the cityscape was impressive. For this era, anyway.

They used to land much closer in, but after burning a number of people alive and squashing quite a few others, the emperor had pleaded with the gods to use more caution and offered to build a special place for them to land farther away. They had agreed, not wanting to seem heartless, but warned they would only comply if there were a chariot waiting whenever they arrived.

Athena walked down the ramp ahead of him and stepped up into the chariot.

"Take us to the emperor," Apollo commanded the driver, an unshaved man who was dressed sloppily.

The driver nodded and said, "That'll be five bronze asses."

"Pardon me?" said Apollo.

"The drive from the Chariot of Fire to the palace costs five bronze asses," said the driver, pointing at a fee sheet that was stuck to the panel in front of them. "Not including tip."

"You realize I'm a god, right?"

"Just doing my job, pal," said the driver.

Athena gave the man a look of disdain. "We could snuff you out of existence without breaking a sweat."

"Better that than getting fired and having my wife nag at me to find another job," the guy said with a shrug.

"That bad, eh?" Apollo questioned.

"You have no idea."

"All right." Apollo reached into his change purse and pulled forth some Roman coins. "I can't let a fellow suffer just on account of me."

Athena's look at Apollo was even worse than she'd given the driver.

"You *do* understand what it means to be a god, right?" she said with a scoff.

"Of course I do, but I've seen Mother nagging Father. I can't have this poor man's suffering through that be on my conscience."

"Fair enough," agreed Athena. "It *is* pretty

horrible."

"Here you go," Apollo said as he handed over the coins. "Ten butts."

"Asses, and thanks, pal."

WHO ARE THEY?

GUARD CLEARLYACHICKUS COULDN'T help but think that the prisoners who had been brought down to the dungeon were on to her. At least the woman was, anyway.

"Psst..." she signaled to her partner, Probius, a very cute guard who had taken her under his wing ever since she'd been accepted into the force. He was easily fifteen years her elder, but he was fit and gentlemanly. Plus, she had rather a thing for older men. "Probius, any idea who they are?"

"No," he said in a whisper, keeping his eyes on the wall in front of him.

"No word from the upper ranks?"

"No."

"Oh, come on. You always hear—"

"Please leave me alone, Clearlyachickus," Probius said pleadingly. "Last time I got into one of these long discussions with you, I ended up getting reprimanded by Dickus Headus."

That was true. Supreme Guard Dickus Headus was a stickler for duty. There was to be no fraternizing with the prisoners, no discussions amongst the guards, and no women anywhere within eye shot, unless she was a prisoner. It was him that Guard Clearlyachickus always feared because he could have her removed from duty if he ever found out her true gender.

"I think the one woman is on to me," she said and then caught herself, remembering that Probius, too, was unaware of the real situation.

"You're not dragging me into a discussion," he said tightly.

It was a constant struggle for her because she wasn't exactly what you would call uncurvy. In fact, she was quite voluptuous. This made it challenging to tape everything into place each morning and to stuff herself into the standard guard outfit. She also had to keep her hair cropped tightly, not get manicures, and avoid any form of makeup, which was the worst because dark eyeliner really brought out her pale green eyes.

But if that prisoner saw through the disguise, certainly others did too. Right? They must have. Especially since she was the only one playing at this game. Sure, there were a few of the guards who were chubby, but none of them in a feminine way. Well, maybe Guard Dudus Lookuslikealadius, and possibly Guard Manboobius.

"Probius?"

"I'm ignoring you."

Clearlyachickus swallowed hard and then said, "Is there anything in particular that you think that woman may have noticed about me?"

"It's like you just don't care," Probius said with a huff.

"Seriously, we've known each other for quite a while now and I need you to be honest with me."

"I wish you would stop saying things," he said at full voice. "You're going to get me in trouble."

"Guard Probius," Supreme Guard Dickus Headus called down in his haughty voice, "would you come hither, please?"

Probius looked away from the wall and at Clearlyachickus. It was not a happy look. It was the kind of look that conveyed that he was very unhappy. It was the kind of look that made Clearlyachickus tingle.

"Damn it," he said. "Thanks a lot, Guard Clearlyachickus."

"What did I do?" she replied innocently as he stormed up the stairs.

NOW WHAT?

ARTHUR WAS BEING careful not to let his gown touch anything. He was well aware that dungeons were intended to be untidy and uncomfortable, but this was pathetic. The smell alone made him wonder how the torches that were encased behind latticed metal containers didn't explode. There were rats and bugs, and it was warm and damp. The lighting barely illuminated chains on the walls, a ceiling that was dripping what he could only hope was moisture from the humidity, and a floor that was an uneven mix of dirt and stone.

"This place is disgusting," said Bors, wiping away a drop of water that had landed on his head.

"And it smells terrible," agreed Kay.

Gaheris inhaled deeply. "Reminds me of home."

"Your home smells like urine?" asked Kay with a wince.

"Think of who you're speaking to, Sir Kay," Bors

reminded.

"Oh, yes. True."

"Something doesn't add up about all of this," said Merlin as he sat on one of the stone benches. He obviously didn't mind the filth. "That emperor's name…" He trailed off.

"Flaccidus?" said Galahad.

"Yes. It's wrong."

Galahad nodded. "On many levels."

"No, I mean I don't recall there being an emperor with that name."

"Well, his real name was Longus Dongus."

"None by that name in lore either, Sir Galahad," noted Gaheris.

"Exactly." Merlin took off his hat and began twirling it. "I wonder if we've ended up in a parallel universe somehow."

"A what?" Arthur asked, thinking certain he'd never heard this term before.

Merlin plopped his hat back on and stood back up, walking to one of the far walls. "I have to think."

Everyone else stood around, except for Gaheris, who took up Merlin's vacated seat. He, too, didn't mind the grime. To be fair, it was more likely that the grime minded him.

"What the shet is a parakeet university?" Arty said, finally. "I didn't know birds went to school."

"No," corrected Galahad. "It's a parallel universe."

"Oh," Arty said with a look of understanding. "That's different, then."

Arthur was surprised by this. "You know what they're talking about, Arty?"

"Not a clue."

"It's an alternate timeline," explained Galahad with a sigh.

"Well, that clears it up," said Arty, rolling his eyes. "Thanks fer yer keen explanation."

By now, Guinevere had stepped into the fray and was standing with her arms crossed. She often did this whenever she was irritated, seeking knowledge, or both. Usually when she was irritated, though, she was staring at Arthur. Since she was clearly looking only at Galahad, Arthur assumed she was in a learning mood.

"What exactly does that mean, Sir Galahad?" she asked. "And please use terms we can understand."

"Yes, ma'am. It's kind of difficult to explain, really." He scratched at his beard thoughtfully. "I don't even fully understand it myself. I've just started reading about it recently, truth be told."

"Do your best," instructed Guinevere.

This was another thing she said quite often to Arthur.

Galahad closed his eyes for a few moments while bouncing his head around. It was as though he were rehearsing what he was going to say.

"Imagine that there are two of you in existence," he said, peering out at Guinevere from a squint.

"I like it already," said Arthur.

Nobody laughed.

"You can't see the other one," continued Galahad. Then he began making hand gestures as he spoke. "They can't see you either. But you both exist. Your lives will be the same to a point, but they'll also be vastly different. This is because the other you couldn't have made all of the exact choices you made, nor could all of the people who have influenced your world or your particular life have influenced theirs in precisely the same way."

"Have ye been drinkin', man?" said Arty. "I dinnae see a flask aboot, but if'n ye have some to share—"

"King Arty," admonished Guinevere, "if you don't mind?"

Arty's shoulders dropped. "Sorry, lass."

"Now, Galahad," she said, "how many copies of me exist, exactly?"

"There are likely an unlimited number, my lady. All of them with different lives, different thoughts, different feelings..." He shrugged. "But they're all you, in a manner of speaking."

"Sounds like a pile of horse dung, if you ask me," stated Bors.

"Agreed, Borsy," said Kay, which was not surprising considering he nearly always agreed with Bors. "It goes against all that we've been taught in the church as well."

"That it does," Galahad agreed. "I fully admit that it's quite difficult to believe. I'm merely telling you what I've read."

"You realize that a man could be sentenced to an eternity in hell fire for even imagining such thoughts," said Kay.

"Equally hard to believe," replied Galahad.

"Where did you learn of this, Sir Galahad?" Guinevere asked.

"Just one of Merlin's many books."

Merlin had moseyed back to the group and was listening to the end of Galahad's lecture.

"They were all given to me by Allison," the wizard said. "The thing that Galahad is discussing is known as *Rope Theory*."

"*String*," Galahad amended.

Merlin looked at him. "Hmmm?"

"*String Theory*."

"Ah, yes, that's it."

Guinevere was nodding slowly. Arthur had little faith that she understood their words any more than he did, but then again she always did have a way with seeing things outside the box.

"And how does this knowledge help us in our current situation?" she asked.

"I don't know that it does, Gwen," answered Merlin. "I'm just worried that if this emperor isn't in our native dimension, there may be many other things that are out of whack."

"If it's not our dimension," said Guinevere, "could our other selves be living here?"

"No," said Galahad. "We are far in their past."

"Oh, that's right."

"Sorry to interrupt," interrupted Arthur, "but if none of this is helpful, why are we discussing it?"

Merlin scoffed at this. "Science is always helpful, Arthur, even if it doesn't solve the particular problem at hand."

"Can I say somethin' now?" asked Arty, raising his hand.

"Yes, Arty?" said Guinevere.

Arty looked from face to face as if building up the courage to spit out what was on his mind. Arthur guessed that it was really Guinevere he was worried about. Clearly he was a man who was also married to a woman who had the upper hand.

"Yer all batshit loony," he bellowed. "Talkin' aboot bunches of people bein' the same and all that. Everyone knows there's only one of ye, unless ye've got a twin or somethin'. Besides, that ain't after helpin' us get out of here, is it? Nay, we need to be after settin' up a plan."

"He's right," said Galahad.

Arty had his finger up and wagging in Galahad's face, but it gradually slowed down its pace and then lowered. Arty was left with a confused look. "I am?"

"Not everything you said, no. Just the part about us needing a plan."

"Oh."

"Anyone have any ideas?" asked Arthur.

"We could do a play for the emperor," suggested Bors, going with his mainstay solution for everything.

"Jolly idea," agreed Kay... of course.

Arthur fought not to sigh. "And how would that help us?"

"Get on his good side, obviously," Bors answered.

"Well, it may help the rest of you," Arthur said, pondering the situation, "but I'm doubtful it will save Arty and me."

Merlin reached out and put his hand on Arthur's shoulder. "Kings make sacrifices all the time."

"For their own lot, yeah," agreed Arty, sniffing. "You ain't me lot."

"True, Arty," Arthur said. "This isn't your fight. I must do this alone."

"No," Guinevere stated. "There has to be another way."

"Actually," Arthur said, gazing into his wife's eyes, "this may be the only way. If I speak with this Flaccidus fellow alone, maybe he'll agree to let you all live."

"What about you, Arthur?"

"As Merlin said, my love, kings must sometime make sacrifices."

"No," Guinevere said as her face lost all color. "You can't do that."

"I'll die by your side, sire," Gaheris announced, standing back up.

Arthur thought certain he heard the stone bench release a breath of relief.

"No, Gaheris," Arthur said gently, "you won't."

Gaheris stood firmly. "I die where I die."

"That's true," noted Merlin.

"This is not up for debate, Gaheris," said Arthur, putting on his most kingly voice. "You'll be needed to protect the others."

"Even Bors and Kay?"

"Of course."

Gaheris appeared downtrodden. "As you command, sire."

As if the air in the room weren't thick enough, their conversation stagnated it. Even the torches seemed subdued by the revelation that Arthur was about to face his demise. But Merlin was right. Kings had the good life for a time, but there was always a moment of truth, or many moments of truth, where the king must stand and face the wrath of another in order to protect his people. This was Arthur's moment. It was odd that it had to happen in an era that wasn't even close to being his own, but a kingdom of six was just as deserving as a kingdom of six thousand.

"I'll not stand for this, my husband," Guinevere said, breaking the silence. "Merlin, you must do something."

"What can I do, Gwen?" Merlin said desperately. "We're in a dungeon. You know my magic is nothing but technology, and I have none of it with me that would aid in this."

"Galahad?" she said. "You've studied!"

"Sorry, my lady."

Guinevere spun towards Arthur. "I won't allow it,

do you hear—"

"Dear, listen to me," he said, gripping her shoulders. "We've always known that we must be prepared to give ourselves for our people. It's what we were born to do."

"Ah, damn," said Arty as Arthur and Guinevere embraced. "Why'd ye have to go an' get all honorable?" He groaned for a few moments and then waved his arm in a wide arc and slapped himself on the leg with his hand. "All right, I'll go with ye."

"No, Arty, as you said—"

"Screw what I said. I'm just as kingly as yer after bein'. I can't rightly let ya die alone."

"Honestly, Arty," Arthur said, "I can't ask you to do that."

"Who says ye did? It's me arse, not yers, and I'm after makin' up me own mind as to what it does."

Arthur nodded his head at his fellow king. "You're a good friend, Arty."

"Aye," Arty said, looking away. "Let's get this shet over with."

MERLIN'S HOUSE

DOONAN WASN'T SURE what to make of this Knight Bedivere fellow. He seemed honorable enough, especially the way he'd handled that merchant who had been trying to force the turkey leg down Doonan's throat, but for a man of such regard to be sloshing through town with a hangover was not very soldierly. Well, at least not as it pertains to the reputation of a Knight of the Round Table, anyway.

They had made their way up a small hill outside town where a cliff face stood. It wasn't the biggest crag Doonan had ever seen, but it was the first one he'd ever sighted that was painted in the fashion of a tree.

Bedivere pushed a little button beside the door a few times. A punchy little song played each time. It was more than a bit unnerving to Doonan as magic was not something he found comforting.

"I wonder why he's not answering?" said Bedivere.

"The wizard?" Doonan said worriedly.

"Yeah. I mean, I guess it is pretty early, but he usually is going to bed just about now."

"But the sun's up."

"Your point?" said Bedivere, shielding his eyes.

Doonan sighed. "I've got none worth sharin'. You English sure is different."

Bedivere looked at Doonan for a moment and then shrugged while nodding. At least he hadn't tried to argue the point. Fact was, the English *were* different. They wore full battle gear instead of kilts, appeared to stay up all night drinking, and acted nonchalant about things like missing kings.

The knight reached again for the magical button, but instead knocked on the door.

It opened slightly.

"Well, that's odd," said Bedivere.

"It's opened," Doonan said with a gulp.

"You saw that too, eh?"

Doonan couldn't help but think that the knight had said that sarcastically.

"Are ye makin' fun?"

"Absolutely," Bedivere replied and then pushed the door open. "Merlin?" he called out. "Merlin, are you here?" He took a step inside. "It's Bedivere. You here? I sure could use some of those little pills that get rid of hangovers."

"He's after havin' pills to clear the fog after a bout of drinkin'?"

"Just helps with the headaches, really," said Bedivere. He then held his hand out to stop Doonan in place. "Stay here a moment." He took two steps toward the back room and then stopped and looked back. "And trust me when I say that you don't want to touch anything."

Doonan glanced around, seeing all sorts of fascinatingly terrifying items. There were lights with no flames, a ball with miniature bits of lightning bouncing around in it, and a stack of books that had all forms of designs on them.

"I wouldn't dare," he whispered. "Probably has some curse on this place as it is."

"Uh, yeah, sure," said Bedivere as if Doonan were an imbecile. "Well, let me look in the back."

It wasn't right for a man of Doonan's status to be standing in a place like this. The hairs on the back of his neck were standing on end and his throat was dry. He'd faced the blade of an enemy more than once in his life as a soldier, but that was nothing compared to this. A blade was tangible. It was held by another man or woman and it poked at you. Simple. Physical. Reality. Magic was another beast completely. It was run by demons, and there was nothing simple about demons.

"Doonan," Bedivere called, causing Doonan to jump, "come on back here."

"Ye sure?" Doonan called back.

"Yes."

"I'm fine where I'm at, so unless you really need

me, I'd rather—"

"You want to find your king or not?"

"Aye," Doonan replied as he started walking, cringing with each step.

He turned the corner and found Bedivere standing by a desk of some sort. On it sat a glowing rectangle that had words and images covering it. To the right was a disk-shaped floor that was connected to a semi-hollowed rock face.

"I'm not likin' this," Doonan said as his heart thumped. "What the shet is that?"

Bedivere glanced over. "Looks like a big circle in the ground to me."

"Aye, I can see that. What's it for, ye think?"

"I don't know but there's this magic flashing panel over here. Has numbers and such on it."

"Yeah, I was after seein' that, too. What are ye doin'? Don't touch it!"

"Why not?" said Bedivere, hesitating.

"'Cause ye've no clue what it'll do, ye daft bastard!"

Bedivere laughed. "Why is everyone so afraid of magic?"

"Hmmm, let's see," replied Doonan, adopting a sarcastic tone of his own. "Maybe it's 'cause it can make yer pee sting, cause her tallywhoosit to itch like something mad before it falls off, and it can give ye a fever ye won't soon forget!"

"I think you just described an STD, not magic," noted Bedivere.

"What's the difference?"

"Right," said Bedivere, blinking. "Well, this bit of the screen clearly says, 'Tap here,' soooo—"

"Noooooo!"

WHY ARE WE HERE?

MRS. SMITH, LANCE'S new mother-in-law, had arrived to watch Mitch, Jr. while Allison and Lance headed back to rescue Arthur and the gang. She was a middle-aged woman who gave a clear indication of what Allison may look like as she grew older. Lance was not unpleased. He liked the white hair look, after all.

"I appreciate you watching little Mitchy, Mother," Allison said as she continued typing away at her computer.

"Yes," agreed Lance, "it is most kind of you, Mrs. Smith."

"It's no problem," Mrs. Smith replied with a bit of an edge. "I can always play bingo some other night."

Allison looked up from her screen. "That sounded sarcastic."

"Did it?"

"Mother, what's wrong?"

"Dear," said Mrs. Smith, "it's just that you had many potential suitors who would not have caused a situation requiring you to go back into the Roman era. Yet, you chose one from the Middle Ages." She then looked over at Lance. "No offense."

"I understand, Mrs. Smith."

And he did. The fact was he was out of his element in this future, and it showed. The only things he'd mastered in his brief time in this era were the microwave oven, light switches, the shower, opening and closing blinds, the dishwasher, how to order pizza, and changing a diaper. He'd also learned how to use the television remote, but that seemed more of an innate skill with men… at least that's what Allison had told him.

"I truly doubt you understand, Lance," said Mrs. Smith, though not unkindly.

"We've been through this many times, Mother," interjected Allison. "None of this was planned. It just sort of happened, and Mitch and I felt that it would be best for Mitch, Jr. for us to marry. That's all there is to it."

"And we love each other, too," noted Lance.

"Hmmm?" said Allison, and then, "Oh, yes, that too, of course."

Lance sighed. "I suppose it's true what all of those soap operas say about romance being dead in this day and age."

Mrs. Smith did a quick shake of her head as if surprised. "You watch soap operas?"

"Not much else to do around here during the day."

"Which is your favorite?"

"I'm not good with names," admitted Lance, "but I think it's 'As the Globe Spins' maybe?"

"Close enough. We should compare notes."

"I would like that," said Lance emphatically.

"A lot of my friends have a weekly get-together where we discuss the shows and what we think will happen." She looked him over again. "Maybe you could join?"

"Honestly?"

"Sure, why not?" she said with a shrug. "It would be nice to have a man's point of view." She frowned. "Never thought I'd hear myself say that. Anyway, we go right after doing a bout of mall walking. Good for exercise." She must have noticed Lance was giving her an imploring look, because she rolled her eyes and said, "...yes, you can go with us on that, too."

Lance clapped his hands. "Thank you so much, Mrs. Smith. That would be lovely."

"If you ladies are done planning," said Allison as she walked to the door, "we should really get going."

"Huh?" said Lance, looking up. "Oh... Right."

§ § §

The trip over to the office was quick since they lived only a few blocks away. Lance had gotten used to the sound of cars and the garb of other pedestrians, but he kept to his standard wear of the Camelot Age, which wasn't too far off considering how close they lived to the medieval dinner theater. Allison had mentioned a few times that she would like to take him out for clothes shopping, but she was always caught up in her work.

The portal room was the same as he remembered. Desks everywhere, lighting in the ceiling behind mostly opaque coverings, and a large platform where they had arrived from the past originally.

"I've already uploaded everything to the computer here and it should be all set," said Allison as she studied the screen and pressed a few buttons. "Hop up on the platform and I'll join you in a second."

A few moments later, they were both on the transporter, waiting for the system to go through its standard processes.

First were the lights glowing on the floor like one of those TV shows Lance had watched from the seventies. It was called *Soul Truck* or something like that. It played music that was definitely not what Lance would have thought he'd enjoy, but he had to admit his foot tapped to the rhythm more than once while viewing. Next, the hairs on the back of his neck began to flutter, and then the hair on his head started lifting up. He looked at Allison and her hair was flying all over the place.

Finally, there was a rush of sound, a massive tingling sensation, and everything disappeared.

An instant later, the sights and sounds came rushing back in and they found themselves standing in Merlin's transporter room with Sir Bedivere and a man Lance did not know. He was a red-haired fellow who was wearing a skirt. Well, it was a kilt, but it looked to Lance like a skirt.

"What happened?" said Allison, looking more irritated than confused.

"Bedivere?" said Lance, feeling a little groggy. "That's you, right?"

"Lance?" replied Bedivere. "I… uh…"

The red-haired man was in a fight-or-flight stance. "What kind of devilry is this?"

"We should be in Rome," Allison said frantically as she hopped off the platform and began reviewing the screen at Merlin's desk.

"Rome?" said Bedivere.

"Get ye back or face me blade," said the kilt-wearing man as he pulled an axe out and held it menacingly.

"Who is this?" Lance asked Bedivere.

"One of King Arthur's guys. From Scotland. His name is Doonan."

"Oh," said Lance, the fog finally clearing from his thoughts. "Nice to meet you, Doonan."

Doonan's eyes blazed. "My steel will meet your demonic loins."

"What?" said Lance, grimacing.

"I don't understand what happened," said Allison, throwing up her hands. She then squinted at

Bedivere and pointed. "Did you touch that screen?"

Bedivere pointed, also. "That screen?"

"Yes."

"No."

"Are you sure?"

"Yes."

Allison moved past Bedivere, coming close to Doonan.

"Get ye back, witch! I'm not fond of strikin' the lasses, but I shan't be vexed by your curses!"

Lance reached over and snatched the axe away from Doonan as if it were nothing.

"Calm yourself, man."

"He has the strength of an army," Doonan said with a look of awe, his open hands shaking.

"No," Bedivere said, laughing, "he's just a knight, and you were looking the other way."

"Oh. Well, I still have me knife—"

Allison stood up and put a hand on her hip. This was the universal sign that told a man he was in trouble.

"I'm not a witch and this isn't devilry. It's just technology. Honestly, you're like a caveman."

"I am not," Doonan said, looking hurt.

"Then why all the talk of devilry and witches and demons?" countered Allison.

"Because ye just went after poppin' out of thin air, is why! How are ye after explainin' it without the use of magic?"

"Via a time dilation chamber that drops our

bodies to a molecular structure, places them into a convecting oscillator with…" She paused. Doonan's face had gone completely white. "What's the matter?"

"Are ye even speakin' English anymore?" Then he gulped. "Or is that witch-speak?"

Lance, who was now mildly used to the idea of time travel and technology, couldn't help but feel bad for the Scotsman. Bedivere seemed slightly uneasy too, but he was known to hang around with Merlin from time to time, so even he appeared desensitized.

"Right," said Lance. "Any idea what happened?"

"Yes," replied Allison. "Bedivere tapped on the screen here and interrupted our transport."

Bedivere looked affronted.

"I did not."

Allison went to put her hand back on her hip, which caused Bedivere to point at Doonan.

"He did it."

"What?" said Doonan. "I dinnae no such thing!"

"Do you two have a habit of going around and touching other people's things?"

Doonan got a serious look on his face. "Not since I had me therapy."

"I don't believe that's what she meant," said Lance, taking a step away from the Scotsman.

"Oh."

"Why are you here, anyway?" asked Lance.

"That's after bein' a deep question," answered

Doonan at length while rubbing his chin and looking up thoughtfully. "The Great Lulach said it's all about findin' yer soul mate. 'Course he spent his days in prison after bein' arrested for pinchin' ladies on the bottom. The Not-So-Great Mac Bethad claimed that we're here to worship the way—"

"I'm asking why you have broken into Merlin's chambers?" Lance interrupted.

"We didn't break in, Sir Lance-A-Lot," stated Bedivere. "The door was open."

"Fine. Why are you in this room?"

"I was lookin' for me king," explained Doonan. "He came here a bit back and he's not returned." He paused and glanced around. "Dinnae wanna come here at all, truth be told, but that damnable Calle commanded it, so here I am."

"I see."

"Are ye after knowin' where me king is?" asked the Scotsman.

"He's in Rome," answered Allison as she began working the keyboard.

"Rome?" Doonan flinched. "Did he go on a horse or somethin'?"

"Ancient Rome," amended Allison.

"What?"

"It's hard to explain," said Lance, "but let's just say that we're on our way to retrieve both him and *our* King Arthur as well."

With what appeared to be a lot of effort, Doonan announced, "I'm going with ye."

"Sorry, no," said Allison. "You've already seen too much as it is."

"He's *me* king!"

Allison nodded. "So you've said. We'll bring him back to you soon enough."

"Ye can't force me to sit by as me king is off in some faraway land!"

"I'm sure he's fine," Allison said with a dismissive wave. "Just relax."

Doonan stood tall and crossed his arms. "I'm going and that's after bein' final."

"Don't make me put a curse on you," Allison replied nonchalantly as she continued typing.

The Scotsman blanched and gulped. "So we're waitin' here, ye say?"

"Both of you," Lance replied. "Bedivere, stay here and touch nothing. Just go sit on the couch and wait. Keep him there, too."

"Understood."

Lance nodded and then tilted his head at the knight. "You truly do, right?"

"Said I did."

"Right."

THE EMPEROR, THE KINGS, AND THE GODS

ARTHUR AND ARTY stood in front of Emperor Flaccidus. Arthur hated to have to do this, as it *was* his life that was coming to an end, but to save his men, and especially his beloved Guinevere, he would do what he had to do. Having Arty next to him proved that the English and the Scottish *could* be comrades… at least if it all started due to the fact that both kings happened to share in the desire to wear women's clothing, anyway.

"So," Flaccidus said with a satisfied smile, "you have come to beg for your lives?"

"We aint' beggin' fer nothin', ye daft—"

"Arty," said Arthur, putting out a hand to stay the man. "Sorry, Emperor Flaccidwilly."

"It's Flaccidus!"

"Ah, yes, that. We are not here to beg for our lives, but rather for the lives of our comrades."

Flaccidus resumed his smugness. "Is that so?"

"It does you no harm to keep them alive," Arthur explained.

"True. We could always use a few more slaves."

Arthur fought to remain calm. It was better for them to be enslaved and alive than to be hanging from the end of a rope, or worse.

"As you say."

"Either way, you two must perish because—"

Hemorrhoidoclese burst into the room, causing the two guards on duty to pull their swords and prepare for an attack. Obviously they noted it was one of their own, though, and therefore returned the blades to their respective sheaths.

"My emperor, I'm sorry to interrupt—"

Flaccidus turned to the two Arthurs and said, "It really is annoying when they do that, isn't it?"

"Happens to me all the time," Arthur commiserated.

"Aye. Rangy bastards."

"Does he always speak so gruffly?" asked Flaccidus while scrunching up his nose.

"Ye think he speaks with angst?"

"Was talking about you."

"Oh. Aye." Arty didn't shrug or bow or make any move to apologize. He just pushed out his chest proudly and said, "It's after bein' a trait of me people."

"Right." Flaccidus glanced at his guard. "What is it, Hemorrhoidoclese?"

"Appolo and Athena have just arrived, sire."

Flaccidus nearly fell over. "Send them in, man!"

"Yes, sire."

Hemorrhoidoclese snapped his fingers and the two guards by the doors opened them.

A muscular man led the way. He had wavy hair and a swagger in his step that said he knew he was powerful. Even had Arthur not just seen the way Flaccidus responded to the knowledge that these two were waiting outside, it would have been clear this fellow was royalty.

The woman who followed him was beyond gorgeous, but she too was built like a finely-tuned machine. Her movements were like that of a snake, and, were Arthur being truthful, it was a snake he'd not mind being bitten by.

Both the new arrivals glanced over Arthur and Arty as if they were subjects, mere peons. Oddly, under their gaze, Arthur felt as though he were.

"Flaccidus," said the man by way of greeting.

His voice was a bit more flamboyant than his body language, which seemed out of place to Arthur. It was a singsong voice that belonged to someone a little less… manly.

"My god," said Flaccidus from a kneeling position. "It is always an honor."

Apollo removed his hand from the top of Flaccidus's head. "You may rise."

The woman, whom Arthur assumed was also a "god," was pacing back and forth in front of him and Arty. She appeared to be sizing them up. If she were truly a god, they would be no match for her, but Arthur had learned over his years that some people just had to demonstrate their superiority wherever possible. This was when Arthur recalled that he, too, was royalty.

He coughed to himself.

"So King Arthur and King, well... Arthur." The side of her top lip lifted. "Interesting that you're here."

"Are we after havin' met before?" asked Arty.

"We're gods," said Apollo. "We know everything."

"Gods, eh?"

"That's right."

"I ain't after rememberin' hearin' about no god named Apple Hole."

"It's 'Apollo,' you dimwit," said Apollo tightly. "This is my sister—kind of. Her name is Athena."

"Kind of?" ventured Arthur.

"She came out of my father's forehead," explained Apollo as if it were a thing that was commonplace.

"What the shet?" said Arty with a tilt of his head.

"It's a long story," replied Athena, stepping in closer to Arthur, "and probably just a myth anyway. So why are you here?"

"They claim they were at a costume party," answered Flaccidus before either of the Arthurs could respond.

"Explains the lady's outfits," said Apollo in a way that came across as interest.

Athena turned away and seductively walked over to the table where the grapes were sitting. She plucked one from its stem and began rolling it between her fingers. Arthur swallowed as she looked back and playfully touched the grape to her lips, gently pulling it into her mouth with a smirk.

Both Arthurs were nearly drooling by now, as were the two guards standing over by the grapes.

"Is Lance-A-Lot with you?" she said and then bit down.

"Huh…?" Arthur replied dumbly. He shook himself back to reality. "No, why?"

Athena frowned. "Damn. Just heard he has quite a... uh... sword."

"Me word," yelped Arty in disbelief. "The damn thing is so impressive that it's a legend hundreds of years before the man was properly born!"

"How could you possibly know about this?" said Arthur.

"As I said," answered Apollo, "we're gods."

"Right."

Apollo then turned and seductively walked over to the same table as Athena. He snapped up a grape and did the same sensuous play that his kind-of sister had done.

Both Arthurs were wincing at this, as were the two guards standing over by the grapes.

"Flaccidus," said Apollo with a sudden frown, "what is your plan with these men?"

"I'm to have them executed."

"On what grounds?" asked Athena, though Arthur couldn't tell if she actually cared or not.

Flaccidus pointed at Arthur and said, "He's the king of Britain and he's the king of Scotland. Solves our issues regarding conquering them both."

"I see," said Apollo, "but I'm sorry we cannot allow this execution to take place."

"But you must! It's—"

"Don't raise your voice at me, Flaccidus," said Apollo coldly. "I would hate to strike you down."

"Sorry, my god," Flaccidus said quickly, his voice barely audible.

Athena had her arms crossed as well and was giving Flaccidus a very stern look. They definitely had the royalty thing down better than most. Honestly, it was as if they'd invented it.

"Don't forget that we put you in this palace between the normal emperors because you throw a decent party," she said sternly. "You shouldn't be in here at all, and you're already precluded from having a legacy."

"Exactly," agreed Apollo. "You're what we call a stop-gap solution."

"Yes, I know." Flaccidus sighed heavily. "I'm... worthless."

Apollo nodded. "Correct. Now that we have that cleared up, we expect you'll do as we say?"

"Of course, my god."

It wasn't Arthur's place, but seeing a man berated as such was painful to watch. He had subjects who were sometimes naughty, but he would take them aside quietly and discuss the situation, not publicly flog them. There were many kings and queens who loved to humiliate people, of course, but to Arthur's way of thinking it was dishonorable. It was equally dishonorable to stand idly by while it happened.

"Excuse me," he said, raising his arm, "but while I don't know this man very well and while I'm quite certain that we would be dead were it not for your intervention, do you not think that treating him thusly is a bit vexing?"

"No," said Athena as if it were a stupid question.

Apollo frowned and looked up at the ceiling for a moment. "Not at all."

"Harsh," said Arty.

"Thank you for your concern," Flaccidus whispered as he moved over to stand with Arthur, "but, to the gods, an emperor or a king is naught but a peasant."

"I don't treat my peasants with such disdain," declared Arthur.

"Aye, agreed," said Arty. "They'll stick ye with a blade in your nethers during naptime, if'n ye not after bein' careful."

"Enough of this," said Apollo while stomping his foot with each word. "Where are the others in their party?"

"They're in the dungeon, my god," answered Flaccidus.

"Fetch them all!"

THE ARRIVAL

THE TRANSPORT WASN'T as jarring for Lance-A-Lot this time. It had all the same whirring and noises and such, but he didn't feel nearly as foggy. A little, sure, but not bad.

Allison hadn't seemed bothered either. She just tapped him on the arm and pointed at the two guards standing in front of them. They were facing away.

The one on the left was short, chubby, and had graying hair that spelled he was the older of the two. The fellow on the right was lanky and a bit taller. He was probably the height of Lance himself.

"Who are they, do you suppose?" Lance whispered.

"Roman soldiers, I'd guess."

The thinner of the two guards glanced back over his shoulder and then spun quickly, pulling his sword out in the process.

"Two more of them, Buttus Facius."

"How are we not seeing them when they arrive, Thumpus Rumpus?"

"My guess is that we're looking the wrong way."

"But Nameous Oneus and Nameous Twous are just over the hill," said Buttus. "They should have spotted them."

"True, but they're both idiots."

§ § §

On the other side of the hill stood two very plain guards. They were both of average height, average build, had brown hair, brown eyes, and stood at their posts in average stances. They were neither good nor bad at their jobs, but rather, again, merely average.

"Do you suppose we will ever get ahead in life, Nameous Twous?"

"I don't hold much hope, Nameous Oneus. Why do you ask?"

"I don't know," Twous said, kicking at the dirt. "Just always felt like I was meant to do something more, you know?"

"Not really."

"Like I have a destiny or something."

"Hmmm."

The two stood staring at the open plain before them. Behind were the palaces and governmental buildings and large gardens, but these two were never placed in areas that overlooked that. They got the barren horizon view.

"Like what?" asked Oneus.

"What do you mean?"

"Well, you said you felt like you have a destiny, right?" Oneus said.

"Yeah, so?"

"So what do you think it is, Nameous Twous?"

"Ah, I see." He wiped his brow before answering. "I can't quite put my finger on it, but I sense it shall be rather important indeed. Maybe I'll be sent to save a princess, or possibly they'll choose me to lead an army. Something of that sort."

"Hmmm," said Oneus again, nodding sagely. "I hate to be the bearer of bad news, Nameous Twous, but my thoughts tell me this could not be the case for either of us."

"Why not?"

"It's basic logic," said Oneus.

"It is?" replied Twous.

"Of course."

Twous looked back off into the distance for a moment, but then said, "I don't understand, Nameous Oneus, why would we not be utilized in some grand way?"

"Because we were not even important enough for the authors to give us proper names, man!"

§ § §

Thumpus pointed the sword at Lance and Allison. "Anyway, who are you two?"

"I'm Allison Smith."

"And I'm Mitch Bowenkawski," said Lance powerfully, "though you may know me as Sir Lance-A-Lot."

Buttus scratched his cheek. "Let me guess: Costume party?"

"I don't think—"

"Yes," interrupted Allison. "That's right. Were there others here from the costume party? We're looking for them."

"Took them to the emperor earlier," answered Thumpus. "They said they had an invitation. You have one, too?"

Allison smiled. "Of course. We were with them."

"Were?" Buttus said.

"We, uh…" She turned away slightly as if hiding a blush. "We stopped off in the woods for a little afternoon delight."

"Heh heh," said Buttus.

Thumpus winked at Lance and said, "Well done, Sir Lick-Her-Spot."

"That's Lance-A-Lot."

"Ah, yeah, sorry."

Buttus Facius grunted and said, "Follow us."

ALONE TIME

JUPITER AND LETO had finished watching the end of *CSI: Alpha Centauri* and Jupiter was not pleased with the outcome.

"How is it that a Roriorian Nun killed the guy?" Jupiter said, scoffing. "It doesn't make any damn sense. Firstly, it's against their Order to do so; secondly, she wasn't even in the vicinity when it happened; and finally *she was dead before he was!*"

"It's just a show, dear," said Leto as she sat in front of the console to check on the status of things on Earth.

A green light blinked.

"Who is that?" said Jupiter, standing behind Leto.

"*That* is Lance-A-Lot," Leto replied with a grin.

"And who is that with him? She's rather ravenous."

"Probably just some floozy."

"Even better," Jupiter said, grinning himself.

Leto leaned back and glanced coyly up at Jupiter. "You thinking what I'm thinking?"

He was. "Swing party?"

They both began to giggle. It wasn't often that Leto would go in for that sort of thing these days, so whenever she brought up the thought, Jupiter was more than happy to oblige. Obviously there was something about this Lance-A-Lot fellow that revved her warp drive, but if that meant Jupiter would get a roll in the hay with the other woman, he wouldn't complain.

"Whatcha'll looking at?" said Pluto as he walked into the room.

"Nothing!" Jupiter said, spinning away from the console. Then he realized he'd been a little too animated. He leaned back on the desk and scratched on its corner. "Nothing at all."

"Hmmm."

"So," Jupiter said at length, "you going out tonight, by chance, Pluto?"

Pluto looked at him curiously. "Wasn't planning on it. Why?"

"No reason. Right, dear?"

"Nothing I can think of…" Leto trailed off and then held up a finger. "Except maybe judging the dead or something?"

"What?"

"You know they call you Hades and you're supposed to judge the dead?"

"Yeah, I know," he said with a shudder. "Never

did like that. Kind of creepy."

Jupiter could see that Pluto needed a little more of a hint. The one thing men shared was the ability to tell when one of their pals had the potential to get lucky. It was an unwritten rule that, when spotted, your duty was to vamoose as deftly as possible.

"Anyway," Jupiter said, giving Pluto a knowing look, "was just thinking it may be a nice night for you to be... somewhere... else."

"Sorry?"

"You know," Jupiter said, more insistently, "*go somewhere else* on this fine evening." Then he winked and added, "Like, away from the ship, for example."

Pluto frowned. "What are you talking about?"

Leto sighed and pushed Jupiter out of the way. She then stood up and put her hand on her hip. Both gods flinched.

"We want to bone," she stated. "So go away."

"Oh!" Pluto nearly choked on his drink. "Well... Wow! Uh…"

Leto pointed at the exit to the landing bays. "Now!"

"Jeez," said Pluto, setting his drink down and walking to the door. "Is she like this during your—"

"Now!"

"I'm going, I'm going!"

ALL BACK

THE ENTIRE ENTOURAGE from Camelot was back up in the main palace.

Arthur quickly detailed what had transpired between him, Arty, the gods, and Flaccidus. The fact that neither of the kings were going to be executed was a relief for everyone, especially the kings who were planned to be executed.

Things were a bit more relaxed now, too. They were all seated and there were small plates of fruits being passed around. Arthur would have preferred a nice bowl of stew and an ale, truth be told, but he wasn't going to press his luck.

"All of you are from a different time, yes?" asked Apollo.

"Well, uh—" started Merlin, giving Arthur a concerned look.

Apollo waved at the wizard. "Speak, Merlin."

"You know my name?"

"Of course," Apollo replied with a chuckle. "We're gods. Right, Athena?"

"Though it should be abundantly clear by now," she said tiredly, "I shall answer it once again: Yes, we're gods."

"Uh, okay," said Merlin. "Well, are you sure you want me to speak of this in front of Fickleweenus?"

"For the love…" Flaccidus closed his eyes and took a deep breath. "My name is Flaccidus, man! Honestly, how difficult is that to remember? Don't you think it's bad enough of a name as it is?"

"Sorry," said Merlin with his hands up in surrender.

"He's just a temporary emperor," Apollo said dismissively. "Who is he going to tell?"

Galahad leaned forward. "Temporary?"

"Of course," said Athena. "Any of the scholars from your day can tell you there's no Emperor Flaccidus in the history of the Roman Empire."

"I was originally Longus Dongus," Flaccidus put in.

"No one cares," Athena said, clearly getting a good deal of enjoyment from the man's humiliation.

"Harsh."

"Truly, it is," Arthur agreed with Arty. He then set down his bowl of fruit and focused on Athena. It wasn't much of a challenge since her beauty was unfathomable. "What have you against this man?"

"He killed off his brother because of a lost bet," Athena answered.

"Horrible thing to do," spat Apollo.

Flaccidus looked at everyone in turn. "He made me change my name from…" He stopped and put his head in his hands. "Oh, never mind."

Arthur had seen many lives taken during his years in royal circles. There was always some enterprising person who had designs on ruling an empire. They rarely understood that to be the ruler put you square in the crosshairs of a slingshot, bow, crossbow, knife, or sword. And if you were in the future, there were also pistols, sniper rifles, and all sorts of advanced explosives—based on the shows he'd seen on Allison's TV, anyway.

"So," Arthur began, "because he had his brother killed—which is indeed dastardly, unless it was for a solid reason, such as protecting the kingdom—you dislike him?"

Athena raised her eyebrows and said, "His brother was great in the sack."

"So true," said Apollo wistfully.

"Amen," agreed Slutius.

Flaccidus snapped his head towards his queen. "What?"

"Okay," Merlin said, obviously having had time to think things through during the discussion over Flaccidus's, well, predicament. "We came back in a time machine."

Apollo nodded sagely. "Is that so?"

"We saw you arrive," noted Athena, "but we weren't sure how you'd done it."

"Indeed. Did you invent this contraption, Merlin?"

"No, Apollo. I haven't a clue how it works."

"Do any of you know?" asked Athena.

Nobody said anything. They all just shook their heads. Merlin and Galahad probably *did* know something about it, but they were being tight-lipped. Surely the gods could manage time travel. If not, how would they know about Arthur, Merlin, and the rest? There were no future books. Speculative novels, sure, but nothing like a history book of the future.

Arty grunted finally and said, "All I know is that it involves bein' in a cave that's after lookin' like a tree."

"What?" said Apollo.

"It was in my house," answered Merlin. "I live in a hollowed-out cave. Anyway, apparently something went wrong and we ended up here."

"I see, I see." Apollo flicked a grape into the air and expertly caught it between his teeth. "You do realize that this could jeopardize your timeline, right?"

"I'm all too aware of that," Merlin replied, "but I'm afraid we are rather stuck."

They couldn't have been stuck for too long. Allison would have to notice something was awry the moment that she and Lance came back for a visit. That was some time away, sure, but as long as these gods were about, it seemed that Arthur and his party were safe.

"Flaccidus," commanded Athena as she stood and stretched, "prepare a feast for this evening so that we may discuss this further. Put our guests in proper lodgings and keep a set of guards around to protect them from prying eyes." She began a sensual walk to the main door. "I shall be in the main suite."

"Mine?" said Flaccidus.

"Is that a problem?"

"Uh…" Flaccidus's shoulders drooped. "No, my god."

"Didn't think so."

"And I shall be at the bath house," announced Apollo with a wide smile.

Flaccidus sniffed. "Not surprising."

"What was that?" Apollo said, stopping and looking back at the emperor.

"Uh… Was just thinking about who to invite to the feast."

"Good point," Apollo mused. "Too late to get local royalty roused."

"Invite the lower level guards," Athena said wickedly. "Tell them to dress for a night of fun. Make their superiors walk the walls for once."

"Devious," giggled Apollo. "I like it."

"They'll be furious, my god," Flaccidus yelped, looking weaker with every passing moment.

"Would you prefer the fury of your elite guards," Athena said as her eyes grew cold, "or mine?"

WHERE'D THEY GO?

AS THUMPUS RUMPUS and Buttus Facius walked Allison and Lance down toward the emperor's palace, Lance took the opportunity to look around.

There were large buildings in most directions with some outcroppings of empty areas splitting amongst them. Each structure was impressively put together with gigantic cylindrical columns, grand steps, and carved artistry that demonstrated the skill of the craftsmen from this age. The people were mostly dressed in white outfits that revealed their legs and arms. They wore thin leather belts that appeared to serve no real purpose besides decoration, and Lance was hard-pressed to spot anyone unadorned with jewelry.

The two guards were walking ahead of them, obviously taking the ruse of Lance and Allison being invited guests to heart. Were Lance in their shoes, he would have followed his quarry so that he could keep an eye on them.

"So how long have you two been guards?" asked Allison.

Thumpus glanced back over his shoulder and answered, "Going five years now for me."

"I'm just about four myself," said Buttus.

"Enjoy it?"

"Better than when I was a towel-boy at the bath house," replied Thumpus.

"What was wrong with being a towel-boy?"

"I was on the male side."

"Ah."

"My last job was okay," said Buttus as they walked down a few steps. "Was a taskmaster."

"What's that?" Lance asked.

"Like it sounds: I yelled at slaves and hit them with a whip when they didn't work hard enough." Buttus shrugged. "Did that for years, but sort of lost the joy in it. It was fun enough at first, sure. I mean, think about it, I was getting *paid* to yell at people all day and hit them with a whip. But I couldn't help but wonder if there was more to life than that."

"And did you find that 'something' in being a guard?" said Allison.

"Not in the least."

"Dignitaries," Thumpus announced.

They stepped off the path for a few moments as a procession of people marched towards them. Each was wearing a gold-leafed tiara, all of different sizes and shapes, and they all had younger servants bumbling behind them who were carrying scrolls and leather pouches.

As each set walked past, Lance was able to hear brief snippets of their conversations.

"…And the regency is to make this proclamation when?" said one pompous-sounding fellow.

"Third week of the month," answered another.

A chubby fellow was saying, "Did you see the way Scabbus Scratchus was digging at himself during our discussion? I swear the man is unwashed."

Lance quickly scanned the flock of important figures to try and spot who this Scabbus fellow may have been. As fortune would have it, the man was only a few in line behind the chubby man who had been saying derogatory things about him. Lance knew this because the guy was giving his groin a full-on scratch.

"Did you see how Slipus Outicus's hindquarters were showing from his outfit again?" said Scabbus Scratchus. "You'd think he'd feel the breeze."

Lance glanced back up the line. Sure enough, the man known as Slipus Outicus was displaying his derrière for the world to see.

"Let me ask you, Dribblus Mucus," queried a strong-looking brute to another who was busily wiping his chin, "do you honestly think we can have the crops sewed up by the end of the season?"

"It can be done, Uranus Bleedus," answered Dribblus. "We just need to stay focused."

Lance found these names odd, but as he watched them pass, he cringed. Some people should simply *not* wear white.

"How are the kids these days, Fukus Toomuchus?" said a man to one of the few women in the group. "You have, what, fifteen now?"

"Seventeen, Rotundus Posterius," the woman replied.

The marching paused, giving Lance a good view of the man, making clear that his name fit his persona as well.

"How do you keep track of them all?" asked Rotundus with a chuckle.

"It's all in how you name them."

"What are their names again?"

"The oldest is Vini, and then there's Vini, and Vini." She was counting on her fingers while looking up to the right in thought. "Vini, Vini, and Vini. Then Vini, of course, and Vini, Vini—"

"Wait a moment, Fukus Toomuchus," said Rotundus, "you keep saying the same name over and over again. Did you name all of your children Vini?"

"Ah, yes, sorry I didn't explain that. When I was listing them off just now, I was recalling their faces and not thinking of the actual names. You see, when you have so many children it just doesn't make sense to name them all differently. Doing that means that I'll have to call them all to dinner by each name. With seventeen kids, that's a challenge." Fukus Toomuchus smiled proudly. "For me it's easy. When

I want them to all come to dinner, I merely holler out, 'Vini, it's meal time!' and they all come running."

"Brilliant," said Rotundus, to which Lance had to agree. "But, Fukus Toomuchus, it begs the question what do you do when you only wish to speak with one of them?"

"Oh, that's easy," she replied with a dismissive wave as the line began moving again. "If I have need to discuss something with only one, I just call them by their last name."

"Ah," said Rotundus Posterius.

Lance had to think about that one for a minute.

Soon they were back on the path and heading towards the palace again.

The weather was hot, but dry. While he wasn't exactly uncomfortable in his getup, he assumed the guards must have been on fire. That was the life of a soldier though, and one that he'd spent many years serving himself. In their own way, they were undoubtedly proud of the fact that they were suffering with sweat. Plus, it gave them something to complain about at the end of the day.

Lance felt an odd sensation at that moment. A tingling. He glanced over at Allison and saw her hair was sticking up. Something was wrong.

§ § §

"What level did you make as taskmaster, Buttus?"

Thumpus asked, feeling somewhat impressed.

"Seven."

"I didn't know that. You were pretty near the top. Upper management." Thumpus studied the gruff, middle-aged man as they continued walking. "I'm impressed."

"Yeah, but they wanted to push me up that final step, running an entire section."

"Seriously? You could have been a Vice Taskmaster?"

"Was within reach," replied Buttus, "but I wasn't interested in doing the hours. I like having my evening and weekends. Plus, giving reports to the emperor isn't exactly my idea of fun."

"I'll bet. Well, anyway, as you can see, we've both been guards since—" Thumpus looked back and paused. "They're gone."

"What?" replied Buttus, spinning around. "Shit."

"Where'd they go?" Thumpus said, scanning the area frantically.

"I don't know," Buttus said, looking equally shocked.

Thumpus pulled forth his blade, not sure what else to do. If Supreme Guard Dickus Headus heard about this, they'd be walking nightshift for a month!

"We have to find them," Thumpus said as he started to walk away.

"Orrrr…" Buttus said, grabbing Thumpus by the arm, "we could go back to our post and act like we never saw them in the first place."

"That would be dishonest," said Thumpus, blinking.

"Would you rather be honest and deal with Dickus Headus, or turn a blind eye, get home on time, and *not* be punished?"

Thumpus felt his jaw drop. "Wow, Buttus, you really *were* in upper management!"

GOTTA DO SOMETHIN'

SITTING IN THE house of a wizard was not something your average Scottish soldier wanted to do. Aside from the fact that just sitting around was dull, there were also the magical trinkets in the room to contend with.

Doonan was still trying to come to terms with the two people who blinked in and out of existence in the back room. He could see that Bedivere wasn't any better off for having seen the event either. If nothing else, they had that in common. Well, that and being in an army, anyway.

"I can't be after just sittin' around whilst me king is in jeopardy," Doonan said, pushing off the couch and stepping to the window. "It ain't right."

"I'm sure he's fine," Bedivere said. "Merlin goes on these things all the time. Never quite understood how he'd disappeared before today, and still don't really *understand* it, but he's clearly got magic on his side, so I'm not worried."

"Well, I am," stated Doonan. "Magic makes me short hairs curl."

"Of that we can agree."

Bedivere stood up and started walking around as well.

The view out the window was nice. It was a clear image of the castle and the hills beyond. Doonan wasn't a man who traveled much, at least not in a leisurely way, but now and then he got to see visions like this and it made him wonder if maybe it wouldn't be a good idea to take his wife on a trip. Nah, she'd just ruin it with her incessant nagging. Hell, he'd never have joined up in the army had he not married her. Of course, he could go on a trip and just tell her it was a special mission from his commanding officer. He smiled at the thought.

"I wonder if he has a bottle of spirits around here," said Bedivere.

Doonan felt his bladder threaten to loosen. "Ye mean ghosts?"

"No," Bedivere said, looking at Doonan as if he were stupid. "I mean booze."

"Booze?"

"Yeah, that's what Merlin calls it." The knight suddenly grinned and reached into a cubby on one of the desks. "Ah, here's something!"

"You shouldn't be touchin' things."

Bedivere wiped the bottle and studied it for a second.

"Tequila?" he said with a conspiratorially raised eyebrow.

"Ta kill who?" he replied slowly.

"This stuff is called tequila. I've shared many bottles of this with Merlin over the years. Really good stuff. Care for some?"

"Is it magical?" said Doonan with a gulp.

Bedivere nodded. "After about the third glass."

SWINGING WITH THE GODS

A BLINK LATER and Lance was standing inside of an odd place. It wasn't anything that Lance had seen before, but he'd heard descriptions of something like it on the television.

It was cold, had panels and screens everywhere, lots of silver accents, and white floors. The air was conditioned similarly to Allison's apartment, which felt nice compared to the heat of the Roman walkway.

Lance found that he wasn't as freaked out as he should have been. Maybe all of this traveling through time over the last little while had calmed him, or maybe his brain was so fogged from the transports that he was simply incapable of reacting as he once did.

"What just happened?" said Allison in a relaxed voice.

"I don't know," Lance replied, "but I have a feeling we're not in Kansas anymore, Two Toes."

"It's 'Toto' and you really need to stop watching so much TV."

"Actually, wait!" Lance said as a moment of clarity swept over him. "Now that you mention it, I saw something like this on *Ancient Anuses*!"

"Aliens."

"What?"

"The show is about aliens, not anuses."

"That's right. Aliens. Sorry."

Just then a man walked around the corner. He was a big man with gray hair that was set just so. He had steely blue eyes and a nice mid-summer tan. Next to him stood a younger woman who was built pleasingly. She had long, dark hair that accentuated her green eyes beautifully.

"Well, hello there," said the man in a deep, resonating voice.

Lance jumped between his beloved and the fellow, ready to defend her with his life. Truth be told, he would have done that for anyone. It was in his training. But there was something more deep-seated about it with his wife. In other words, it wasn't simply a duty-bound response.

Allison, though, was not like the women of Lance's time. She considered male chivalry to be more of a nuisance than an endearment. She'd told him so many times, in fact. So he wasn't all that surprised when she smacked him on the back of his head and pushed him out of the way.

"I can take care of myself, thank you very much."

"Sorry," Lance replied while rubbing his head.

"Who are you?" Allison asked the gray-haired man.

"The name's Jupiter. And you are?"

Allison's eyes opened widely. "Jupiter?"

"Now that's a coincidence," said Jupiter. "I thought I was the only one with that name. Truly something, don't you think, Leto?"

"She was only verifying your name, dear," said Leto with a commiserating roll of the eyes at Allison. Leto then turned and batted her eyelashes a couple of times before saying, "Hello, Sir Lance-A-Lot."

"What's going on here?" said Allison. "Are you two being for real with the names? I mean…" She paused and looked at Lance. Then she ran over to one of the panels and looked down for a moment. Finally, she turned and walked back slowly. "Holy shit, you *are* being for real."

"Yes, dear," said Leto.

Lance felt smart this time. Usually Allison was way ahead of him on things, but since he had nothing to do but watch TV on most days (and nights), he had learned a ton of things that Allison called "pseudoscience."

"You two are a couple of anuses, right?" he ventured with a proud smile.

"Excuse me?"

"Pardon?"

"Aliens, Mitch," Allison corrected.

"Oh, right, that."

"Who is Mitch?" said Jupiter, glancing around the room.

"That's my real name," said Lance.

"Ah," said Jupiter. "Mine's Zeus."

"No effing way," shrieked Allison.

Lance was not used to seeing her respond like that, except when they were in the bedroom, of course.

"I'm being for realz," said Jupiter.

Allison scrunched her face. "'For realz?'"

"Sorry, it's how the kids talk these days. Was just trying to be cool, you know?"

This had obviously been too much for Allison because she began shaking her head and waving her hands. Her actions made Lance feel as though maybe he *should* have been more apprehensive about the situation.

"Hold the phone," she said. "You two are really the Greek and/or Roman gods?"

"You know it," Jupiter replied with a wink.

"This is unreal!"

"It gets better," added Leto.

"How could it possibly get better?"

Leto began twirling her hair in her fingers. "We've brought you up here to make a bit of a proposition."

"Oh?" said Allison.

Jupiter stepped over and took Allison's hand. He

gave it a kiss, which was the gentlemanly way to greet a lady, so Lance held himself in check. Still, the man held that kiss a little longer than was polite, at least to Lance's standards.

Finally, Jupiter resumed his standing position and whispered, "Ever been with a god before?"

"Hey now," said Lance, stepping forward, "I'll kick you square in the stones and—"

And that's when Leto seductively touched his arm. "You've not been with a god either, right, Lance?"

"Uhhh…" He tried to answer, but whenever his nether region got word that potential action was about, the blood in his brain began to lower, making him far more foggy than what the transporter did to him.

"I'm in," stated Allison without flinching.

Lance's brain quickly reassessed the situation. "What?"

"What, what?" his bride said with a shrug. "How many people can say they've boned a god?"

"Most of the people in ancient Rome right now, actually," admitted Leto.

"True," agreed Jupiter.

"Okay, fair enough," Allison conceded, "but I mean since Ancient Greece and Rome."

Lance was confused. On the one hand, Leto *was* exceedingly hot, and they were obviously in some kind of spaceship, which meant this was one woman —or god, as the case may be—he couldn't possibly conquer—sexually speaking—in either his native era of Camelot or his new one with Allison. Especially not the new one. Still, Allison seemed to have jumped at the chance pretty quickly.

"Are you saying you really want to do this?" he asked.

"Oh, come on, Lance," Allison said as if it were nothing. "Leto is *hot*! Even I can see that. Don't act like you don't want to tag her."

"You're not so bad yourself," Leto said sweetly.

"Ravishing," Jupiter agreed, still holding Allison's hand.

"Lance," Allison said with those puppy-dog eyes she sometimes got, "a god just called me ravishing. I can't walk away from that!"

Lance wasn't very comfortable about all of this, but it wasn't like he could compete with a god, right?

"Well, if you're sure—"

"Sweet," said Allison, smiling at Jupiter. "Let's do this, Zeus."

"Technically, it's Jupiter."

"Right, I get that," Allison said, nodding, "and no offense, but I'd rather screw a god than a planet."

PREPARING FOR THE FEAST

GUINEVERE WAS FINE with going to a feast, but she had nothing to wear. While she rather liked the feel of the boxers and trousers she had on, she didn't feel it was befitting to represent her kingdom, regardless of the era she was currently in. And she certainly didn't think Arthur's green gown was proper for a king to wear to such an event.

Arthur, of course, was busily looking at the architecture in the room. He seemed to be fascinated by the silliest things.

"You seem distant, my petunia," Arthur said after setting down a carving of a cat.

"I don't have my wardrobe, so I feel poorly about joining a party like this."

"You look fine, my love."

"Fine?" Guinevere said, grimacing. "Whatever happened to the days of 'ravishing' and 'picturesque?'"

"You still are, of course," Arthur said, taking her into his arms and then tilting his lower half away. "It's just rather trying to say that when you've got a sock stuffed in your pantaloons."

She nodded. "Fair enough."

"And what of me?" Arthur said, motioning to himself. "If I go down wearing this same outfit, they'll wonder why when there is clearly no costume party happening."

Guinevere was just about to suggest they check for chests and drawers when a knock came at the door.

"Yes?" said Arthur, answering it.

The two guards who had been stationed with them in the dungeon were standing outside, holding outfits that looked similar to those worn by people in this era.

"Pardon our interruption, sir. I am Guard Probius and this is Guard Clearlyachickus. We have brought a change of clothes for you and your lady."

"Oh?" Arthur stepped aside. "Come right in."

Probius and Clearlyachickus stepped into the room and set the clothes at the edge of the bed. Clearlyachickus glanced over at Guinevere a few times, visibly uncomfortable. Guinevere was surprised by her name, thinking maybe she'd heard it wrong. It *was* a her, obviously… right?

"Excuse me," said Guinevere, signaling the guard over.

"Yes, my lady?"

"You're uh—" Guinevere said, suddenly wondering if it was really a wise thing to bring up.

"Yes?" Clearlyachickus said again.

Guinevere glanced at Probius and lowered her voice. "I noticed you in the dungeon. What's your name again?"

"Guard Clearlyachickus, ma'am."

"Clearlyachickus?"

"Yes, ma'am."

"And yet you're dressed like a man."

Clearlyachickus's eyes looked like something Allison had referred to as "a deer in headlights."

'What are you saying?" said Clearlyachickus.

"You *are* a woman, right?"

At this, the guard swallowed hard. She looked over her shoulder at the other guard. Guinevere gazed past the woman as well. Probius was standing facing the headboard of the bed, obviously doing his best to not hear a thing.

"You can tell?" whispered Clearlyachickus.

"Sorry," answered Guinevere with a nod.

"Is it my knockers? I try to tape them, but they're rather—"

"Enormous, yes," said Guinevere. "And, 'knockers'?"

"It's the outfit," the guard replied. "I speak that way when wearing it for some reason."

"I totally understand." Guinevere spun around slowly. "You'll notice I'm wearing men's garb myself."

"I *did* notice that, but I thought you were at a costume party."

"Right, well, my point is that I find myself saying man-terms as well in this getup."

"Ah." Clearlyachickus had the sudden look of finally meeting another person who could understand her predicament. "I also keep my hair short and I try to wear loose clothing when off-duty, but these leather guard outfits make my booty pop."

"And you clearly shave your legs," noted Guinevere.

"Oh, damn," Clearlyachickus groaned. "Didn't think of that."

"*And* your name is Clearlyachickus."

The girl furrowed her brow. "So?"

"Say it aloud."

"Clearlyachickus," she said. "Sorry, I don't see the problem."

"Seriously?" Guinevere said. "Okay, what is a chick?"

"A baby chicken."

"Ah, yes, I suppose it depends in what time you're in, then," said Guinevere, and then added, "and probably locale. In my time a chick is the same thing, but way in the future, it's a name that men call women."

"The future?"

"Yes, we call men 'dudes' or 'guys' and they call us 'babes' or 'chicks.'" She then tilted her head to the side. "Well, not all of them, but you get the idea."

"Not really."

Guinevere felt for the girl. It was bad enough hundreds of years in the future, but she imagined it was even worse in this time. Then again, from looking around at the people here, it may not have been.

"Do any of the other guards know?"

"I don't think so," she said uncertainly.

Guinevere snapped her fingers at Probius. "You there: Is there anything different about this guard when compared to other guards?"

"What are you doing?" hissed Clearlyachickus.

Probius stepped over, keeping his eyes firmly ahead, looking at neither of them.

"In what way, ma'am?"

"Let's go with physicality," said Guinevere.

"Guard Clearlyachickus is the same as all guards, as far as I can tell," Probius replied without inflection.

"Is that so?"

"We're taught to see no differences in each other, ma'am."

"So there is *nothing* you've noticed that's out of the ordinary with Guard Clearlyachickus?"

"Except for the large knockers and bouncing booty, you mean?" Probius said, speaking precisely as he was expected to.

"Yes, except…" Guinevere crossed her arms and gave him a duck-look. "No, that's exactly what I mean! Doesn't that strike you as odd?"

"It strikes me as the only reason I tolerate getting sent to Dickus Headus all the time," admitted Probius and then snapped his eyes back to the wall.

"What?" said Clearlyachickus.

"Who?" said Guinevere.

Probius began to sweat. "Uh..."

"Wait a second here," Clearlyachickus said, stepping in front of Probius. "You *were* assigned as my partner, right?"

"Yes, of course... Sort of... I mean..." His shoulders dropped along with his stare. He sighed heavily and said, "Not exactly."

"I'm confused," Clearlyachickus said.

"I asked to be on duty with you whenever possible," Probius admitted.

"You did?"

"I did."

"But why?" Clearlyachickus questioned. "I always get you in trouble. I don't *mean* to, but it seems to happen anyway."

"You honestly don't know?" he asked, staring into her eyes.

"No."

"It's because I'd rather look at your physicality, as she put it, than at the other guys. Besides, you smell nice. The other guards just smell."

"Probius! I never knew you knew I was a woman."

"Seriously? Your name is 'Clearlyachickus.'"

"Right."

"Everyone knows," Probius said after a second. "I'm just the only one who pays Dickus Headus to let me... Uh—"

"You *pay* him?"

"Oh boy," said Probius, wiping the sweat from his forehead.

Arthur broke the tension by walking into the room, parading around in his white outfit. He had a spring in his step as he pirouetted a few times.

"What do you think?"

"That's the female outfit, sir," stated Probius.

"Oh?" Arthur replied innocently.

"Arthur," warned Guinevere while shaking her head, "go and change into the proper one, will you?"

Arthur smiled mischievously. "Sorry, my persimmon."

"Maybe we should get out of your way," said Probius while turning briskly towards the door.

Clearlyachickus was hot on his heels. "Guard Probius, you and I seem to have a few things to discuss!"

AFTERGLOW

WHEN LETO AND Lance had finished up their fun-time, they headed back out to the main area of the ship.

Lance couldn't quite pinpoint the way he felt other than excited. Not because he'd just boned a god, though that was pretty fantastic, but because he found the entire concept of being on a ship in space rather incredible. Obviously most people would be thrilled to be in his position—and many would also have loved being in the position that Leto was in less than thirty minutes ago. But others from his era would have been terrified—and, yes, that relates to *either* of the aforementioned positions… Leto was quite adventurous, after all.

"That was amazing," Leto said, swooning as they rounded the corner, "and now I know why they call you Lance-A-Lot." She giggled. "Come to think of it, that's the first time I've called a man 'god.'"

Jupiter and Allison were seated on opposite ends of the couch. Jupiter's face was downcast and Allison had her arms crossed. She was wearing a frown of disappointment.

"Was your tryst as lovely as mine, dear?" Leto said, clearly oblivious to the tension in the room

"It was, um…" Jupiter cleared his throat. "Things didn't quite progress as…" He adjusted in his seat. "You see, I felt a little bit of pressure and—"

"He couldn't get it up," announced Allison.

"Yes," Jupiter said, slumping even farther, "that."

"So why didn't you take your Godagra pills?" asked Leto.

"I can't, ever since starting the blood pressure medications," he replied. "You know that."

"Oh, that's right."

"So you two didn't have relations?" asked Lance.

"Nope," replied Allison. "Seems I wasn't enough of a draw to get a god horny enough."

"Oh, don't think that," Jupiter said desperately. "You're quite attractive for a non-god. I'm just not as young as I used to be."

"A non-god?"

"I feel just terrible about this and…" Jupiter paused and looked at Lance's mid-section. He pointed. "Are you trying to steal something from my ship, you pathetic human?"

Lance looked down. "Excuse me?"

"A ray gun, maybe?" Jupiter said, standing forcefully. "One of our advanced batteries, per chance?"

"Jupiter, will you relax?" said Leto. "That's just his dong."

"Oh, sorry." Jupiter instantly seemed to calm down. "I'm just a bit overwhelmed at the moment and…" His face contorted again. "*That's his dong*?"

"Part of it, anyway."

Jupiter groaned. "Well, I'm sure *that* won't help my performance issues." He turned to Allison. "Honestly, I don't know what you were expecting, dear, but I don't even think a horse could compete with that."

"So I'm learning," replied Allison.

"You are quite lucky, you know?" said Leto with a forlorn look.

Allison gave Jupiter a sideways glance. "Again, so I'm learning."

There was a chiming sound that reminded Lance of the phone ringing in the future. This one played a tune that he hadn't recognized, though, and it seemed to be sounding throughout the ship.

"I'll get it," said Jupiter as he reached for a small, black circular piece that he then pressed into his ear. "Jupiter here. Oh, yes, Apollo, what is it? A feast? Okay, well, I think your mother and I will stay on the ship. You know we only like to make an appearance during dire times." He nodded a few times. "True, true, but I'd rather you and Athena manage this one on your own. We'll send down the latest two arrivals from the future. Hmmm? Oh yes, Allison Smith and

Sir Lance-A-Lot showed up a little while after you left." Another few nods. "Right, well, I must go now."

"What's going on?" asked Allison.

"Your friends are apparently the guests of honor at a feast this evening, so you should really get going."

"The sooner, the better," said Allison as she got up and walked to the place that they'd arrived at earlier.

"Again," Jupiter attempted, "I'm truly sorry that things didn't... work."

"Sure. Right. No problem."

Jupiter groaned miserably.

"I'll transport you down to the main chambers," said Leto. Then she glanced again at Lance's middle-region and sighed wistfully. "I should probably make sure the batteries are at full charge first... on many things."

"What?" said Jupiter.

Another man walked in, saying, "You all done yet?"

"Your timing is as impeccable as ever, Pluto," Jupiter said with a sour look.

"Pluto?" asked Allison, looking him over.

"My lady," Pluto said, kissing her hand.

Allison glanced back at Lance questioningly.

"If you feel you must, dear," Lance said, sighing.

"What's this about?" Pluto asked.

"Ever bone a human before?" Allison said with a

wink.

"Many times, yes," Pluto replied, letting go of her hand.

"Well, then?"

"Uh, I mean you no offense when I say this, lady," Pluto said uncomfortably, "but you're not my type."

Allison's face tightened. "Oh, yeah? Well, you're not even considered a planet anymore!"

CAUGHT

ARTHUR FOUND THE male version of the Roman outfit to be nearly as fun to wear as the female version. It was white, loose-fitting, had a nice rope-style belt, and hung somewhat like a skirt, showing off his legs. The sandals felt a little strange, but he had to admit they complemented the outfit perfectly. His favorite bit, though, was the gold-leafed tiara.

It was also nice to see Guinevere wearing a womanly outfit again, but he wouldn't dare say anything to her about it. He would also have to be careful to avoid words like "ravishing" and "picturesque" so that she didn't get a complex.

"Ready, my sweet?"

"I suppose," Guinevere replied, clearly not as happy in her current outfit as Arthur was in his.

They opened the door to find Guard Probius and Guard Clearlyachickus going at it all hot-and-heavy.

The two were so intertwined that it was difficult to tell where one of them started and the other one ended.

"Oh, wow," said Guinevere as the two guards jumped away from each other. "Can't say I expected that."

"Ah!" Probius said in shock. "Sorry, my lady. We were... I mean—"

Clearlyachickus attempted to clarify things. "It's just that, uh—"

"How unprofessional," stated Arthur, feeling quite vexed. In all of his years as a king, he had never witnessed anything like this, not with guards anyway. Sure, Lance-A-Lot had a tendency of boning everything in sight, but not while he was on duty. "I shall have a word with your emperor about this."

"Oh, Arthur," Guinevere said, hushing him. "No, you won't."

"I shall so!"

She hand-on-hipped him again. "If you do, I'll take away the key to my naughty clothes cabinet."

Arthur blanched. "You wouldn't."

"Try me."

"Fine," he said with a pout. "I won't say anything, but if you were my guards, you'd be flogged for this breach of protocol."

"No, they wouldn't," Guinevere noted.

"Well, no, but they'd be whipped, at least!"

"Nope."

"Stuck in the cells for a month?" he said

hopefully.

"Not even that."

Arthur squared his shoulders. "A firm talking to, then, with accusatory pointing and everything."

"Okay," Guinevere conceded, "you'd probably do that."

Finally Arthur had gotten the upper-hand... sort of.

"He's actually quite an old softy," Guinevere said as she looked back at the newly formed couple.

"Let's not bring *that* into the discussion," Arthur replied, nearly choking.

"I was talking about your demeanor, dear."

"I know you were talking about da wiener and I don't appreciate—"

"*Demeanor*, dear," Guinevere interrupted, giving him one of her looks.

"Oh, right."

"Anyway," Guinevere said, "why don't you two take our room for the next couple of hours?"

"We're on duty until we deliver you to the party, ma'am," said Probius. "After that we're supposed to be *at* the party."

"Well, it'll take you a few minutes to change, right?" Guinevere then chuckled. "And after all that you two have been holding back over the years, I'm sure a few minutes is all you'll need."

Clearlyachickus arched an eyebrow. "Devious."

"You have no idea," agreed Arthur with a sigh.

TAKING CHANCES

DOONAN WAS NOT one to take chances, unless you include touching ladies' bottoms without their consent as chancy, which the local authority in Scotland had. He'd not done anything nefarious beyond that, of course. It wasn't in his nature. Even when he had pinched a cushion or two, it had been done as sneakily as possible.

But after having a few glasses of this tequila that Bedivere had given him, he was feeling adventurous.

"Want to go down into town and pinch… hic… some bottoms?"

"What?" said Bedivere.

"Uh, nuthin'."

"I got an… hic… idea," Bedivere said.

"What's that?"

"Why don't we go and use that magic-screen thing in the back?"

"For what?"

"To... hic... to... hic... to see what it does."

It didn't sound as pleasant as pinching a tail or two, but Doonan was feeling bored. There was something in the back of his mind that told him this wasn't the greatest idea, but the alcohol convinced him otherwise.

"Ooookay," he said, following Bedivere to the back room. "Now what?"

"You stand on that platform... hic," Bedivere said, "and I'll do something on this screen."

"Like what?"

"I dunno." Bedivere giggled as he tapped all over the screen. "There, that should do it!"

"Do what?" asked Doonan.

"I dunno."

He pressed the big red button on the screen and the ground began to flash under Doonan's feet.

Run, you fool! his subconscious said, but his conscious mind was so muddled that it heard, *This is fun, it's cool!* and so he stayed in place.

An instant later he found himself standing in a field surrounded by gigantic trees. The sky was blue with wisps of red and it was hot and humid. The grass, where there was grass, appeared to be smashed down in places. It looked as if gigantic footprints had crushed the green stems into the ground.

He heard a snort and spun around to see an enormous lizard standing not two hundred feet away. It stood ten-men high, had teeth the size of

Doonan's arms, a head that was easily four times his size, and arms that were tiny and swinging pointlessly at chest-level.

Doonan froze in place as the thing seemed to survey him from afar. It was clearly aware of his presence, but Doonan didn't know what to do, especially since his mind was still swimming from the batch of tequila he'd downed.

He gulped as the air grew still.

Suddenly, the massive creature roared so loudly that Doonan grabbed his ears and shat his pants.

It began running at Doonan with such speed that there was nothing the Scotsman could do but empty his bladder too.

Just as the beast was upon him, its wide jaws closing in on snapping Doonan in two, the world flashed and he was back in Merlin's house.

"What… hic… happened?" said Bedivere. "And… hic… what's that smell?"

Doonan couldn't answer verbally. It was all he could do to breathe.

"Well, what?"

He pulled his hands up to make them look as small as possible and then he bared his teeth fiercely.

"What the hell are you doing?" said Bedivere. "Oh wait… hic … Is this charades?"

Doonan nodded.

"Got it. How many words?"

Doonan held up four fingers.

"Four. Okay… short arms and… hic… vicious

teeth," said Bedivere as Doonan resumed his stance. "Hmmm, sounds like some kind of creature, maybe?"

Doonan nodded.

Bedivere stroked his beard thoughtfully. "A kitten?"

Doonan frowned.

"You're right, that makes no sense. Ummm… ooh!" The knight spun and looked at the screen. "Says here you went back… hic… a couple thousand years." Bedivere turned back with wide eyes. "Dinosaur?"

Doonan nodded.

"Wow." Bedivere gulped and then grimaced. "How is that four words?"

Doonan spun around, lifted his kilt, and showed the seat of his underpants.

"Oh, I see," said Bedivere, nodding. "You were doing… hic… charades to answer my 'What's that smell' question, right?"

Doonan nodded.

"But four words?"

Doonan jumped off the platform and croaked, "I shat me pants."

He then grabbed the bottle of tequila, downed the rest of its contents in one shot, and headed off to clean himself up.

BACK TO THE GUARDS

LANCE AND ALLISON arrived back at the location they'd originally landed when transporting from Merlin's house. In front of them stood the same two guards as before.

"Hello?" said Allison, jarring the two men.

"Ah," said Thumpus, turning, "there you two are. Now, where'd you run off to? Could have gotten us in a world of trouble, you know?"

"Sorry," said Allison, still having a look of angst. "We were brought up to speak with the gods. Well, we were technically brought up to bone them, but it turns out that—"

"The gods, eh?" interrupted Buttus with a sniff.

"Told ya they were real," Thumpus stated.

"Have you seen one directly, then?" Buttus challenged his partner.

"Well, no, but I've heard stories." Thumpus then motioned to Lance and Allison. "These two just said they were with them, didn't they?"

Buttus shook his head. "You watch too many hand-puppet plays, Thumpus Rumpus."

"I do not," Thumpus responded. "I just watch the one."

"And what's that one called?"

Thumpus mumbled something.

"Sorry, what was that?"

"*Current Aliens.*"

"Exactly!"

"Sorry to interrupt," said Lance, "but we're still supposed to get to the castle."

"It's called a palace," Buttus said, still displaying his emotional glee at having triumphed over Thumpus in their debate. "Honestly, are you all from a different world or something?"

"I'll bet they are," Thumpus said.

Buttus sighed. "And I thought you were one of the sane guards."

"You did?" Thumpus said, looking surprised. "Thanks!"

THE FEAST

THE ENTIRE TROOP was back together again, but for some reason only Arthur and Guinevere were wearing the white outfits. The rest had on guard uniforms, sans the helmet, including Arty.

They were standing in a large hall with an arched roof, flourishes of gold, statues and busts of people that Arthur knew nothing of, though he assumed they were past emperors or dignitaries, and people milling about, having discussions and eating delicacies. It wasn't all that different from the parties he and Guinevere hosted in Camelot, apart from the size of the building and the number of inhabitants.

The line down the hall was rather long, but they had been told to wait because it was the royal announcer's duty to inform the entire room of each person who was making an entrance.

"What the shet are they makin' *us* wait in a queue for?" said Arty sourly. "We're after bein' royalty!"

"It's not our kingdom, Arty," Arthur pointed out, yet again.

"Oh, it ain't?" Arty said in a grandiose fashion that was laced with sarcasm. "Don't ye think I know that, ye dopey Englishman?"

"Hey!"

Guinevere pushed an arm between the two men and separated them.

"Enough, boys."

They glared at each other for a few more moments before Arty looked away.

"Bah," he said. "I'm sorry for speakin' outta turn as such. It's just that these britches they gave me are splittin' me mossy marbles in two!"

"I know what you mean," said Guinevere."

"Ye do?"

"Well, not in this outfit," she said, pointing at herself, "but I've worn a few that have had that effect."

"Ye have?"

Trumpets sounded, as they did every minute or so, causing most people to pause their conversations and look up at the royal announcer.

Hear ye, hear ye! I hereby present Guards Cranius Rectus and Itchus Crotchius.

Conversations resumed as the two guards walked into the pit of activity, gripping wrists and slapping each other on the back. While it may have irritated the supreme guards, as Emperor Flaccidus had expressed concern over, it was abundantly clear that the lower soldiers were getting quite a boost in morale.

"These names are atrocious," Bors announced.

"I wholeheartedly agree," said Kay, unsurprisingly.

"I'm sure their names are fine to them, you twits," Merlin said, looking rather silly wearing his guard outfit while maintaining the pointy hat.

"Says a man who carries the name 'Merlin,'" countered Bors.

"Better than 'Board Up Myanus!'" Merlin retaliated.

Galahad chuckled heartily at this.

"That's 'Bors De Ganis,' and you know it."

"How rude," said Kay.

Arty, who was clearly ignoring everyone else's conversation, said, "And what's with this footwear, anyway? I don't like having stuff between me toes."

The trumpets burst forth again, jolting Arthur the same as they'd done each time they'd sounded. Why they couldn't have just had a soft bell or maybe a firm clearing of the throat, he could not say. Granted, they used trumpets a lot in his day, too, but he'd decreed that it only be done *outdoors*.

I hereby present Guard Horatio Harrassyurass and his wife, Giganticus Mamarus.

"I must use the privy," announced Gaheris.

"You couldn't have gone before?" said Kay.

"I go when I go."

"At least he warned us this time," Galahad said before Kay could argue.

"Oh, come on, then," Bors said, taking Gaheris by the hand as if he were a child. "Kay and I will take him to the loo and come back after all this announcing foolishness is over."

They padded off, dragging Gaheris behind them.

"And don't even get me started on that helmet they were after expectin' us to wear," said the irritable Arty. "As if I'm going to put that blasted thing on me head."

I hereby present Guards Chokus de Chickenus and Drunkus Askunkus.

"The food smells good, anyway," Merlin said as he stepped from foot to foot.

Arthur understood the wizard's movements since the sandals provided little support. The soles of his feet were already aching and he had the feeling his heels would be bruised before the day was over.

But Merlin was right: The food *did* smell good. There was a buffet of meats, vegetables, fruits, and desserts that was setting Arthur's stomach to grumbling. He'd never been one to have a sweet tooth, but his mouth salivated at the sight of the large white cake that sat at the end of the table. It was slowly shrinking in size as people partook of its yumminess, though, so Arthur feared he may not have the opportunity to sample its delights.

"The food *is* intoxicating," agreed Galalad, "but a more pressing issue is on my mind."

"What?" said Merlin.

"How do we get back to our time?"

"Oh, that. Definitely a problem."

Arty began to fidget again. "It's like they purposefully want to make sure yer danglers never meet each other again!"

I hereby announce Guard Tortoise Beats Rabbitus and his escort, Bodacious Bootius.

"The truth is that we may well be trapped here for a while," Merlin stated as they inched forward.

"At least a month," Galahad said. "Allison assured us they'd visit, but that only happens about once a month, right?"

"Before she had a kid, yeah."

"I'm feelin' a breeze, too," said Arty, spinning around. "Is me crack after showin'?"

I hereby present Guards Prematuria Jackulus, Hernia Rupturus, and Roidus Ragius.

"We'll just have to learn to make the best of things until Allison and Lance-A-Lot catch on to what has happened," said Guinevere as she grabbed Arthur's arm and pointed excitedly at one of the flaming dishes.

"Precisely," said Arthur, giving her a nod at the beauty of the dish she'd indicated. "There are many things that we can bring to the table in a world as ancient as this."

"No, we can't," Merlin said soberly. "Remember, anything we do could affect the timeline."

"Exactly," Galahad agreed with a grunt.

"Maybe I've just got this on wrong?" Arty said, wincing. "I'm after gettin' chaffed!"

I hereby present Hottus Totrottus, Tittus Fascinaticus, and Isconstantly Flashingus.

"Well, we can't just do nothing while waiting for them to rescue us."

"Arthur is right," said Guinevere. "Hopefully Apollo and Athena will aid us with our plight."

Merlin scratched his beard. "I'm still baffled they truly exist."

"You don't believe they're really gods, right?" said Galahad, seemingly taken aback by Merlin's words.

"Of course not, you square-headed mongrel."

"Ye'd think they could have used something other than leather, yeah?" Arty asked. "Or at least have been after softnin' the edges."

I hereby present Guards Scratchus Continuous, Sextus Transmitus Disius, Tellus Anotherus, Tinius Weenus, and Hugi Bearus.

They moved forward a bit more. At least now Arthur was able to see the front of the line. If they didn't get to the tables soon, the food would be all but gone. He could only hope there was more being prepared; otherwise, the caterer sorely underestimated how much sustenance it took to feed soldiers.

"What we'll need to do is lay low until Allison arrives," said Merlin. "Talk to as few people as possible, and don't make any suggestions to the people in this era. Even just a simple act of getting two people to talk to each other who never would have before could be catastrophic."

"Truly?"

"It could change everything, Gwen."

"Oh... Hmmm."

"Gwen," said Merlin with a squint, "why do you look concerned?"

Arty started doing short squats. "Pretty soon I'm just gonna take the damn thing off!"

Hear ye, hear ye! I hereby present Guard Ballus Hairus, his wife Nippletonia, and their sons, Forskinius, Pubius, and Dave.

"'Dave'?" said Galahad, looking at the others.

"That's what I heard, too," Arthur said.

"Odd name."

"Not really, Galahad."

"I mean for ancient Rome, sire."

"Ah."

"Gwen," Merlin pressed, "is there something you want to tell us?"

"Not really."

"Okay, is there something you *need* to tell us?"

"I'm sure it's nothing."

"Oh, great," Arty whined. "Now it's startin' ta itch!"

I hereby present Guard Cornus Holious and his wife, Vaginitus.

It seemed as though the line was moving more quickly all of a sudden. Arthur had noticed that one of the supreme guards—at least he assumed the man was a supreme guard since he was on duty— had come up and given a message to the announcer.

"Gwen?" said Merlin.

"Well," Gwen said as they shuffled forward, "it's just that these two guards obviously had the hots for each other and, well, I let them use our room."

"Me feet hurt, me soggy sack's gettin' split, and me taint is after itchin' like the devil," stated Arty. "Am I truly the only one feelin' this?"

I hereby present Guards Muttus Nuttus, Sweetus Parfaitius, Schlongus Longorius, Harrius Palmus, and Rectumus Odiferous.

"Why did you offer them your room?" Merlin said to Guinevere.

"To have relations, what do you think?"

"Oh boy," said Merlin and Galahad in unison.

"Anyone have a tissue or a bit of cloth?" Arty asked.

I hereby present Folatio the Philanderer, Dubius Phallaci, Wankus Maximus, Dropa de Turda, and Senilius... What's that? You're at a party, Senilius. Yes? For the guards. Hmmm? Yes, Senilius, you're a guard. Now just move along, will you?

"Looks like we're up next," said Galahad as they approached the royal announcer, who took the cards they had handwritten their names upon.

Hear ye, hear ye! I hereby present Art Hurr, Gwen of Ear, Gallonhead, Art Tee, and ... Merlin.

"Why'd he only get your name right?" said Arthur as they walked past the announcer.

"How am I supposed to know?"

"Gallonhead is not even close," complained Galahad.

"Oh, shet," said Arty pathetically. "We're after havin' to walk down steps now?"

IT'S A WEAPON!

BORS, KAY, AND Gaheris had returned, lucky to avoid having their names butchered by the royal announcer, and after everyone got their fill of food, they headed over to the table where Emperor Flaccidus, Queen Slutius, Apollo, and Athena sat. There was a group of large guards standing in a semi-circle in front of the table. In front of them were...

"Lance-A-Lot?" said Arthur with a start.

"Allison?" Merlin chimed in.

The guards backed away slightly, allowing the new arrivals to step into the mix.

"Good to see you, sire," Lance said with a nod. He then bowed to Guinevere. "My lady."

"Again," said Arthur tightly, "she's *my* lady."

"Sorry, sire."

"I haven't any idea who these new people are, my love," Slutius was saying to Flaccidus, "but I warn you to be cautious because that one looks to be carrying a club in his pants."

Flaccidus snapped his head back and deftly pointed. "Guards, seize that man!"

"What is the meaning of this?" said Arthur, jumping between the guards and his knight. The other knights, along with Arty, moved into position as well. "Why are you putting guards after this man?"

"He has clearly got some kind of weapon there," the emperor said, pointing.

"Where?" said Arthur, feeling confused.

Flaccidus pointed. "There!"

"That's not after bein' a weapon, ye moronic emperor," Arty said, still wincing uncomfortably from the garb he was wearing.

"Slayed *me* with it more than once," said Guinevere.

Arthur jolted. "More than once?"

"Well, it was the same night."

"Agh! It was bad enough when I'd thought he'd just done it the one time."

"Oh no, many times," Guinevere said proudly. "Just one night. Took me weeks to recover, though."

"Ew," said Arthur, thinking the food he'd just eaten might make an encore presentation. "I don't want to hear this!"

"I wouldn't mind hearing about it," Athena said with a wicked grin.

"Me either, sister," agreed Apollo.

Athena ignored him. "Would rather experience it, though."

"Oooh, snap," Apollo said while moving his head from side to side.

"Sorry, sire."

The Roman guards and the English knights—and Arty, who was so irritated at his current wardrobe situation that Arthur assumed he could have managed the fight all on his own—were staring each other down. It was clearly a losing proposition for the knights, but it was in their training to fight for right.

"I don't understand what's going on here," Flaccidus said, motioning for his guards to back down. "What are you all discussing?"

Arty did another short squat and scrunched his face as though he'd just caught wind of Sir Gaheris's britches.

"Just that the thing in that one's pants," said the Scottish king, "is a different kind of weapon than yer after thinkin' it is."

"What do you mean?" said Flaccidus.

Arty straightened up. "It's his beef cannon."

"Sorry, his what?" Flaccidus replied with a frown.

"Angry cucumber."

"I don't understand."

"His tummy banana."

"Wait," Flaccidus said, "are you telling me that's a piece of fruit?"

"Nay, it's his dangling spout."

"Huh?"

Arty took a deep breath and answered, "His pointy plug, hefty hose, lap club, love python, soldier sausage, dragon dagger, pocket rope, gnarled trunk, stud stilt—"

"You are making no sense at all to me," Flaccidus interrupted, sitting back in his chair while throwing his hands up in surrender.

"Hmmm," said Arty, and then snapped his fingers. "Ah ha! It's his Veinous Maximus!"

"Veinous Maximus?" said Arthur.

Arty shrugged. "When in Rome, yeah?"

"Are you trying to tell me that *that* lump in his trousers is his praetorian penetrator?" said Flaccidus.

"Uh…" It was Arty's turn to squint. "Maybe?"

"Oh," Slutius said with glee. "I see the outline now. Yes, that's not a weapon. I mean, well, it *does* look dangerous. In a good way. A very, very good —"

"Honestly," Flaccidus cut her off, "it's like you just can't get enough. You should have been named Wantsitalot or something."

"Seriously?" said Guinevere. "Her name is already Slutius."

"So?"

"Never mind."

"Anyway," Flaccidus said, setting his hands on the table, "you obviously know these new people, Arthur?"

"We do," answered Arthur. "This is Sir Lance-A-

Lot, another of my knights, and this is his wife, Allison Smith."

"Ah ha," Flaccidus said, pointing sternly at Allison. "So you're the one who had a costume party and didn't invite me?"

"I did?" Allison replied, looking around.

"Just roll with it," Merlin whispered. "We didn't expect you to arrive so soon."

"Oh. Uh, yeah, sure. Sorry about the non-invite." Allison's eyes darted about. "Didn't think you'd be interested."

"Why wouldn't I be?" Flaccidus replied, looking injured by her comment. "I like to dress up and have fun. Just because I'm an emperor doesn't mean I'm a stick-in-the-mud."

"No," agreed Athena. "That would be Apollo."

Apollo sat up. "What?"

"Well," Allison continued, "I'll remember for next time."

"There may not be a next time," said Flaccidus sinisterly.

"All right, all right," Athena said, waving her hands. "Calm down, Flaccidus, and everyone else. These people are under our protection."

That shut everyone up. It was one thing to go against the Roman soldiers, but it was entirely something else to do battle with those whom the Roman soldiers feared.

"I cannae take it anymore," said Arty as he reached under himself and pulled down on the leather strap that had been squishing his nethers.

Everyone cringed at the sight of Arty's junk dangling freely.

"Who the shet made these outfits? This strap is threatenin' to snip off me tenderviddles, it is."

"That's not supposed to go under there," said Athena, giggling. "It's meant for holding a dagger."

"It is after holdin' me dagger!"

"No," she said while pointing around at the other soldiers who had on the same outfit. "See?"

"Damn. I'll be back."

"So what do we do now?" said Arthur as he watched Arty skitter away while reaching under his person to hold the strap down.

"I don't know about the rest of you," said Athena, "but I could stand a little alone time with Lance-A-Lot."

Slutius cooed, "Me too."

"For the love of…" Flaccidus stopped and then just shrugged. "You know what. Just do it. I've had about enough of you anyway."

"Back off, ladies," Allison said, pulling Lance closer to her. "He's mine."

"Excuse me?" said Athena as though Allison was naught but an antagonistic little fly.

"He's my husband."

"So?"

"And he also slept with your mother," Allison said with a look that said she believed she'd just gotten an edge.

Athena's expression contorted. "He slept with my father's forehead?"

"What?"

"Long story," Apollo interjected, "and nobody believes it anyway."

"Wait," Athena piped up again, "are you saying he slept with Leto?"

"Precisely."

"Ew. Well, that ruins that."

"I'm still okay with it," announced Slutius.

"Of course you are," Flaccidus wailed. "You're a damn slut!" He instantly stopped with a look of eureka. "Oh," he said, turning to Guinevere, "I hear it now."

Guinevere gave him a wan smile.

"Right," said Arthur before this could go any further. "Well, seeing that we've resolved *that* issue— though it does always seem to be a point of discussion with him around—what do we do now?"

TIME TO GO

ARTHUR STOOD WITH Arty and Flaccidus near one of the columns. Arty had addressed his wardrobe malfunction, but he was still shifting from side to side and wincing now and then.

Allison and Merlin were busily discussing the transporter technology with Apollo and Athena as Queen Slutius stood over by one of the windows chatting up Sir Lance-A-Lot.

"Don't let him do it," Arty was saying to Flaccidus. "Ye'll be after regretting it for all yer days."

"The way I see it, she'll get it out of her system," Flaccidus replied with a shrug.

"That ain't the problem," Arty replied. "It's the getting it *in to* her system that ye should be worried about."

"Oh."

"He'll not do anything anyway," Arthur said.

"Allison is here, and unless she approves of Lance having relations with another woman, he won't partake. He's honorable that way. When he's single, he's a regular horn dog—to borrow a term from Merlin, but when he has a significant other, he wouldn't dare step out on her, unless, again, she approved of such a deed."

As if on cue, Slutius looked suddenly sad. Lance put a hand on her shoulder for a moment before walking back over to Allison.

"See?"

"Aye," said Arty.

"Whew," said Flaccidus.

"Ye don't know the half of it," Arty said, "and ye'll be damn glad yer wife ain't after knowin' the whole of it!"

"Right," said Arthur as he motioned towards Merlin and the gods. "I'm going to start rounding everyone up."

The discussion that he'd entered was full of words he didn't understand. This wasn't uncommon when it came to speaking with the likes of Merlin, but at least he could ask for definitions during those one-on-one talks. With this bunch bandying about words regarding time travel, computers, and other odd-sounding terms, it was akin to standing with a group of people who were all speaking a foreign language.

"Sorry to interrupt," Arthur said at a break in the conversation, "but we should really be getting back."

"True," Merlin agreed. "We've overstayed our

welcome as it is."

"Actually, how exactly are we going to get back?" asked Galahad.

"I have a personal transport device," she answered, reaching into her pocket and pulling out a small box. "I just need you all to join me in one of the rooms or some other location where it's just us. Then I'll transport to Merlin's house, set up the computer, and have you all transported as well."

Merlin raised an eyebrow. "Clever."

"Comes with the territory."

Arthur took one last look around the hall. It was beautiful, to be sure. He'd almost wished Merlin had brought along one of his picture-taking devices so he could permanently capture the moment.

"Well," he said to Apollo and Athena, "it was definitely an interesting stay."

"Sorry about how Flaccidus treated you when you arrived," Athena said with a frown. "Again, he's just a temporary fill-in until we find someone more fitting for the job."

"He wasn't so bad," said Arthur. "Merely trying to protect his land."

"If you say so."

"He's a boob," Apollo stated outright. Everyone looked at him. "What? He is."

"Right, well, then."

Arthur bowed and stepped away.

Guinevere was speaking with Guards Probius and Clearlyachickus by the main door. The two lovebirds looked to be glowing. While Arthur still found their behavior unprofessional, he couldn't help but appreciate that they'd found happiness with each other. This was especially true because he knew how Guinevere so loved playing the role of cupid.

Probius had more of a relieved look than a joyous one, but Arthur understood that relief was akin to happiness when it came to certain soldiers.

"We have to leave, my persimmon," said Arthur, giving a smile to Clearlyachickus.

"Already?"

"Sorry, dear, but it's time."

"Oh, all right."

She gave Clearlyachickus a prolonged hug, which left Arthur feeling as though he should at least shake hands with Probius.

"Was a pleasure meeting you," Arthur said in a cordial tone.

"And you, sire."

Arthur felt as though he should say something more. He was never one for these awkward moments.

"Uh… may you have lots of success in your life."

"Thank you, sire."

"Uh… and may all of your dreams come true."

"That would be wonderful, sire."

"Uh… and may you have lots of children who grow to do great things."

"Most kind, sire."

"Uh… and may your lineage be great and produce

kingdoms of splendor." He was really reaching now.

"It would be a dream come true, sire." Probius shifted uncomfortably. "My apologies for the lack of discipline outside of your room. It was just—"

"No, no," Arthur said, seeing that the man was woefully distraught over the situation. A king learned over time when a soldier was just playing the game of sorrow—Purcivale and Tristan came to mind—and when he was genuine. "As the pointy-hat wearing fellow over there would said, 'We're good.'"

"Thank you, sire."

"Right." Arthur cleared his throat. "My love?"

"Don't they make a wonderful couple dear?" Guinevere said, glowing.

Arthur peeked over his shoulder again at Merlin. The wizard would not take kindly to Guinevere having been a part of this union. She clearly understood Arthur's worry, too, as she gave him one of those "oopsie" looks.

"And I'm equally thrilled that you helped me to see the light, my lady," Clearlyachickus said. "I'm going to start an underground movement to improve the well-being of ladies everywhere in Rome."

"That's wonderful," said Guinevere, beaming. "Isn't it, Arthur?"

"Uh… yes, of course. Wonderful."

Arthur quickly locked eyes with Probius, who remained stoic. If he were feeling any concern over the words of his new lover, he was hiding it well.

This told Arthur the relationship between these two had a solid chance of success.

"Puddin'," Arthur said again, "we should really be moving along. Merlin is going to start getting—"

"Yes, you're right," she interrupted. "Farewell to you both. I'm sure you'll live happily ever after, as they say."

They padded off to a room where the rest of the troop had gone. It was much smaller than the other rooms Arthur had seen, but it still carried the same style of decor and coloring. Honestly, there wasn't a room he'd seen on this trip that wasn't impressive… aside from the dungeon, of course.

"Good luck to you all," said Athena as she and Apollo stood at the door. "We'll assuredly see some of you soon."

"Looking forward to it," Merlin said, seeming to have changed his mind on the role of these self-proclaimed gods.

The door shut, leaving the original troop, plus Lance-A-Lot and Allison.

"Okay," said Allison. "I'm going to transport to the future and will bring you along shortly. It should only take a couple of minutes." She was about to press a button on a little device she was carrying, but stopped. "Nobody leave this room, understood?"

"I stay where I stay," announced Gaheris.

"We'll be here," affirmed Arthur.

"Aye," Arty agreed. "I'm tired of this shet. I wanna be after gettin' home!"

"Good," said Allison, and then pressed the button.

BACK TO CAMELOT

THE MOMENT THEY returned to Merlin's house, Arty jumped off the platform and breathed a sigh of relief.

"Never thought I'd be happy to be back in this damn tree."

"It is good to be home," Merlin said with a smile. "Also, you may not have noticed, but you two dudes look like kings again."

Arthur glanced over at Arty, seeing the man in his full Scottish outfit. Arty was looking back, nodding and grinning in a way to let Arthur know that he, too, was seeing only Arthur's English garb. Guinevere was dressed in pantaloons still, but she didn't have one of the Rings of Veiling that Arthur and Arty had.

They heard the sound of song coming from the other room. Well, more precisely, they heard two drunken men singing two different songs as if competing with each other.

When they rounded the corner, they found Sir Bedivere standing face to face with a Scottish soldier, both of whom were drinking, laughing, and singing.

"What's this after bein', then, Doonan?" said Arty.

"Hmmm?" Doonan said, looking as though he were having trouble maintaining his balance. "Ooooh, shet. Sorry... hic... sire! They had tequila."

"Ta kill who?" said Arty.

Merlin held up a bottle and tipped it, showing that the contents had been drained. "Tequila. It's a potent brand of booze."

"It's Sir Bedivere's primary skill," Arthur said in accusation, staring at the bottle.

Arty looked at him. "What?"

"Drinking," Arthur answered.

"Same with Doonan," Arty said, "though he was supposed to have had therapy for that... among other things we shan't rightly mention. Now, tell me, ye rangy soldier, what are ye after doin' here?"

"Calle... hic... told me to come up and find ye, sire." Doonan swallowed hard and shook his head. "I seen some things here that I cannae unsee, but I shan't... hic... say a word ter nobody aboot it. Ever. Hic. Trust me!"

"Well, I'll have Ceallache's head on a platter for that. Told him ta stay put, I did!"

Doonan winked. "Ooookay," he said in sing-song fashion.

"Wait a second here," said Merlin, taking off his hat and setting it aside. "Shouldn't we have come back merely minutes from when we originally left?"

"I didn't think it would matter a few days either way," answered Allison.

"How long have we been gone, then, local time?"

"About a week," she answered.

"Oh," Arty said, lowering his hackles. "Well, that's after bein' different, then."

"Ooookay."

"Actually, Arty," Arthur said curiously, "I never did ask you why you came up to visit me in the first place."

"Oh yeah, aboot that. Me wife is throwin' a bash and wanted me to invite ye and yer Nets."

"My Nets?"

"He means knights," noted Guinevere.

"Aye, and don't get started on that," warned Arty. "It's been a long week, yeah?"

"Sorry," said Arthur. "Couldn't you have just sent a messenger?"

"Aye, and after all that's happened, I'll damn sure be after doin' that next time!" He then leaned in and added, "But I wanted to make sure not *all* of your Nets made it. Me queen still fancies another rumble with the human axe-handle."

"Sorry, sire," said Lance, obviously overhearing.

"Do you sleep with everyone?" said Allison irritably.

"Slept with you," noted Merlin.

"True." She dropped her angst. "Sorry, Mitch."

"Well," said Arthur, "we'd be delighted to join your party. Wouldn't we, dear?"

"Of course!"

Arty nodded. "Good, good. Uh—"

"Tell your wife that Lance and I have other plans," Allison said as Arty glanced at them.

"Aye." He then made a "whew" sound. "Sets me mind at ease, that."

"Speaking of having other plans," Allison said, glancing at the metal band on her wrist, "we should really be getting back to little Mitchy."

"Yes, dear," agreed Lance before turning to Arthur. "Sire, I shall return again in a few weeks to do my monthly tour of duty."

"That's fine," Arthur said. "Thanks to you both for fetching us from Rome. I wasn't all that excited to stay there for long."

"It was my fault you got put in the wrong time and place anyway," Allison admitted. "Well, technically, it was Galahad's fault because he kept fiddling with things."

Galahad coughed. "Sorry."

"Lesson learned," she said in a kind way. "You'll get better at it, Gal."

"Thanks, Al."

Allison frowned at him. "Touché."

They said their goodbyes and headed off to the transporter. Arthur would be lying if he said he wouldn't miss Lance-A-Lot. The king could do without certain reminders of the man, but Lance wasn't the lead knight due to his third leg. He was a good soldier who was conscientious and duty-bound.

Everyone stepped out into the waning sunlight.

It was quite a vision. The street below was still bustling with activity as guards marched along the parapets and the alleyways. Fresh baked goods and grilled meats could be smelled even from their perch at the top of the hill, and though Arthur had already been filled to the brink with foodstuffs from the Roman era, he couldn't help but have a craving for a crumpet or two.

"Gah, guh," said Gaheris suddenly.

"What are ye doin', man?" Arty said, stepping away from the large knight. "There's no fight to be had."

"He goes where he goes," Galahad noted before Gaheris could defend himself.

"Vile, it is," claimed Arty.

"Go home and do that, Gaheris!"

"Sorry, sire," Gaheris said to Arthur with a look of shame as he clomped down the hill toward the row of houses that marked the Knights' Quarters.

"Well, we're off to see how the theater is doing," announced Bors.

"Probably falling apart without us," stated Kay happily.

They nodded at each other and then at the rest of the troop before turning to walk down the hill.

"I suppose we should check in on the wives, too," Bors could be heard saying.

"Probably having a blast without us," Kay replied.

Arthur glanced over at the Scottish king. The man looked rather regal with his magical ring hiding his true choice of garb.

"Well, Arty, it was good of you to come. You're welcome to stay longer, if you'd like."

"Nay, I'd best be gettin' back before Calle goes and starts stormin' the walls here."

"Understood."

The two men gripped arms for a moment, needing no words to explain the kinship (and queenship) they shared. It wasn't likely that another reign of two kings from the lands of Scotland and England would ever again exist that could claim to share both a vision of peace and sense of fashion.

"See ye at the party in a few weeks," Arty said with a nod to Guinevere. "Come along, Doonan."

"Ooookay."

"Bye, Doonan," Bedivere called out. "Was fu... hic... fun!"

"Aye, it was," Doonan called back, stumbling as he walked. "Yer after bein' ooookay in… hic… me book."

"Tha...hic...thanks," Bedivere said an instant before his eyes rolled up into his head and he passed out.

After all they'd been through over the last week, Arthur knew things were going to be pretty dull for a while. He needed a break, certainly—they *all* did—but seeing the wonders of both the future and the past made him see the present as mundane. Then again, he had something that neither era had, at least not unless you went inside a medieval dinner theater. He had true knights with true sport and true feasts that none could outdo. Though he did quite fancy the cake from the Roman times.

"I just want to make sure that everyone realizes we can't talk about any of this," Merlin said to nobody in particular.

"Yep," said Galahad.

"Indeed," agreed Arthur.

Guinevere merely nodded, looking off into the distance as a nice breeze blew across the lot of them.

"Off with you, then," Merlin said, shooing them away. "I have to catch some sleep and start figuring out what's falling apart in this area so Galahad and I can fix it."

"Ugh," Galahad said by way of agreement.

As Arthur and Guinevere walked down the path that led to their beloved castle, they held each other's hand. It was nice to know that the peasants couldn't see what he was truly wearing, especially on such a fine evening.

"I think I shall miss that adventure, Arthur."

"Oddly, so shall I, my persimmon."

"Maybe we can do it again sometime?" she said as they turned a corner.

"Never say, 'never,' as they say."

"Indeed," Guinevere said, smiling. "Indeed."

GENE. E. ALOGY

TWO WEEKS LATER Guinevere had reminded Arthur of the appointment she'd set up with one of the new scholars in town. The man's name was Gene E. Alogy. Arthur hadn't bothered to ask what the "E" stood for. Looking at the squat fellow, with his balding head, ruddy cheeks, and disheveled clothing, Arthur guessed "Egbert" would have been fitting. He only thought this because he had gone to school with an Egbert who looked just like the man, with the exception that the younger Egbert had hair.

Typically these types of meetings would be held in the grand chambers, but Guinevere had told Arthur that he needed to be seen among the people more, so they went to Mr. Alogy's place of business instead.

"Please, please," Mr. Alogy said, motioning to the chairs in front of him, "have a seat. I have a lot to show you today."

"Remember that I have a regency meeting in less than an hour, dear," Arthur reminded his beloved.

"I'll keep that in mind, sire," Mr. Alogy replied with an odd look.

"No, I was speaking with my wife, good sir."

"Oh! Right."

The man went back to shuffling papers. He was clearly nervous, which was almost always the case with people who met with Arthur and/or Guinevere. Arthur had always tried his best to calm them down, but it rarely worked.

He turned to studying the room. There were stacks of paper everywhere, a tattered map on the wall that was stuck full of pins, and a painting of a walrus that seemed rather out of place.

"Nice office you have here," Arthur said, attempting to put the man at ease.

"Thank you, sire. I apologize for the mess. I've been working night and day to prepare these documents for you."

"That's a kindness," Arthur replied with a smile. "By the way, what precisely are these documents supposed to reveal?"

The man paused and looked up. "Your ancestry, sire."

"Ah."

Arthur looked over at Guinevere and shrugged.

"It's important to know where we come from, dear."

"I suppose," conceded Arthur, "but I think it's

more important to know where we're going."

"Without knowledge of the past," Mr. Alogy said as he sat the final stack in place and plopped into his chair, "we're doomed to repeat it. Or so they say."

Arthur found it difficult to argue that tidbit. He assumed every era held some of the same dynamics. Kings or rulers of some sort, peasants, soldiers, merchants, chefs, artisans, craftsman, and many other professions.

"What have you found, Mr. Alogy?" Guinevere asked, clearly far more interested in this venture down memory lane than Arthur was.

"Your parents were—"

"You know who my parents were?" said Arthur, instantly realizing what this was actually about.

He'd heard "ancestry," sure, but he hadn't put two and two together.

He'd never known his parents in great detail. His earliest memories were of his father being hauled off to fight a battle for the English Army and his mother handing up Arthur and his sister for adoption. Arthur had only been four years old at the time. He'd searched for years and years, but had never found his long-lost sibling.

"Are they alive?"

"I'm sorry," Mr. Alogy said sadly.

"Sorry, my love," Guinevere said while touching his hand. She then turned back to Mr. Alogy. "Let's jump back to the farthest information you found, and work our way forward. My husband must meet with the regents soon, as he said, and I have a class to attend on the finer points of fist-fighting and drinking ale."

"Fist-fighting and ale-drinking?" said Arthur, shocked.

"Let it go, dear."

"Right," said Mr. Alogy, clearing his throat. "Well, I was only able to get back as far as 72AD. There just weren't very many records prior to that."

Arthur and Guinevere glanced at each other.

"Apparently, there were two guards named Probius and Clearlyachickus—odd names, if you ask me," Mr. Alogy said with a chuckle. Then he looked up and coughed. "Sorry. Anyway, they had a young child named Findus Excaliburus who went off on a search for a magical sword. He never found it, but his search took him to Britain where he met and married a woman named Agnes." He peered up for a second.

Guinevere and Arthur looked at each other with mouths agape.

"Merlin was right," said Arthur.

"And you'll never say a word to him about it," warned Guinevere.

Arthur was confused. "Why not?"

"Because he'll hold it over my head forever, that's why not."

"True," mused Arthur. "He'll do the same with me since I was there when it happened." Arthur then gave Mr. Alogy a strong stare. "That information never leaves this room. Do you understand?"

"Of course, my lord," Mr. Alogy replied firmly.

"Good," said Guinevere as her shoulders relaxed. "Now, continue, if you please."

"Right. Right." Mr. Alogy shuffled his papers again. "Well, uh, Probius and Clearlyachickus had another child by the name of Locatus Dadamnswordus, though his mother seemingly called him Billy."

"Billy?" said Arthur.

"Correct. Now, Billy also set off to find this sword, but failed in every attempt." Mr. Alogy flipped the pages. "Now, he finally gave up his search after marrying a Scottish woman named Liza. At this point, they stopped using the odd names, and had a daughter by the name of Igraine. She never hunted for the sword, though. Instead, she set about building a clothing empire. Mostly blouses, negligees, and things of that nature."

Again, the two royals looked at each other.

"Well, she ended up marrying a man named Gorlois—"

"Is he my father?"

"No, sire," Mr. Alogy replied. "Actually, rumor has it that a man named Merlin—"

"Merlin?"

"Different one," Mr. Alogy said quickly.

"There was another man with that name?" Arthur said doubtfully.

"Anyway, he was friends with this fellow named Uther Pendragon and—"

Arthur sat up. "That's *my* last name."

"Yes, sire."

"Go on, go on!"

"Uh… well, Uther was in love with Igraine, so he asked Merlin to help him put on a disguise so that he could look like Gorlois. He was doing this so that he could bone your mom."

"What?"

"Sorry, sire! I mean, uh—"

"Just continue, Mr. Alogy," Guinevere said, again patting Arthur's hand reassuringly.

"Yes, ma'am. Uther's disguise was a success and he ended up, well, scoring with your mother."

"That's disturbing," said Arthur, no longer certain he wanted to know about his parents.

"Shall I continue?"

"Please," urged Guinevere again.

"Gorlois was killed—"

"How?"

"I don't know, sire. I couldn't find information on that." The man swallowed. "Well, as soon as that happened, Uther married Igraine and they had you and your sister."

Arthur looked up. "What is her name?"

"Anna."

"Is she alive?"

"No, sire."

"Damn it all to hell!"

Arthur launched from his chair and began pacing around the room. There was so much information coming in at him that he could barely process it. His earliest ancestors were the two guards that Guinevere had offered their room to back in Ancient Rome; the next in line hunted for the same sword that he'd finally found, which secured him the title of King in England; and his father had apparently gone through the trouble of dressing like another man in order to have relations with his mother. He also assumed that his father had a hand in the death of his mother's original husband, though he could only hope that wasn't the case.

It was so much to digest that he was struggling to keep his emotions in check.

To make matters worse, there were horns sounding from all over the campus. This often happened whenever diplomats arrived, which made sense seeing that this was the day he was to meet with the local regency.

"Is there more?" he said finally.

"Yes, sire," said Mr. Alogy slowly.

"Spit it out, man," demanded Arthur.

"You also had a brother that nobody knew about."

Arthur felt his jaw go slack. "A brother?"

"Yes, sire."

"Is he dead, too?"

"No, sire," said Mr. Alogy. "In fact, I took the liberty of having a courier run all of this paperwork to him a few days ago. My guess is that he will read them and eventually visit you."

At that moment the door burst open and the smiling face of Scottish Arthur stepped into the room. He was holding his arms out in grandiose fashion. In one of his hands was a wad of paper with a stamp that read "Gene E. Alogy."

Arty's face was lit up.

"Me bruddah!"

Arthur turned slowly towards Mr. Alogy.

"You've got to be kidding."

ROMAN GUARD NAMES

We'd also like to thank the following people for their contributions in helping to name the Roman guards...

(Listed in alphabetical order by first name. Note that there were many names contributed, but these were the ones that received the most votes!)

Allen Maltbie contributed: Cranius Rectus, Itchus Crotchius, Roidus Ragius, Drunkus Askunkus, Rotundus Posteriorus, Bodacious Bootius, and Dave.

Jamie Smith contributed: Tortoise Beatus Rabbitus, Horatio Harrassyurass, Dubius Phallaci, Dropa de Turda, and Hugi Bearus.

John Debnam contributed: Prematuria Jackulus, Hottus Totrottus, and Sextus Transmittus Disius.

John Ladbury contributed: Wankus Maximus.

Joe Simon contributed: Schlongus Longorius, Harrius Palmus, Rectumus Odiferous, and Chokus de Chickinus.

Mark Brown contributed: Slipus Outicus.

Nigel Brett contributed: Uranus Bleedus.

Noah Sturdevant contributed: Giganticus Mamarus and Isconstantly Flashingus.

Scott Reid contributed: Tinius Weenus.

Steven Palfrey contributed: Tittus Fascinaticus, Hernia Rupturus, Scratchus Continuous, Scabbus Scratchus, and Dribblus Mucus.

Teresa Cattrall Ferguson contributed: Tellus Anotherus, Folatio the Philanderer, and Senilius.

ABOUT THE AUTHORS

John P. Logsdon

John was raised in the MD/VA/DC area. Growing up, John had a steady interest in writing stories, playing music, and tinkering with computers. He spent over 20 years working in the video games industry where he acted as designer and producer on many online games. He's written science fiction, fantasy, humor, and even books on game development. While he enjoys writing lighthearted adventures and wacky comedies most, he can't seem to turn down writing darker fiction. John lives with his wife, son, and Chihuahua.

On the web: www.JohnPLogsdon.com

Christopher P. Young

Chris grew up in the Maryland suburbs. He spent the majority of his childhood reading and writing science fiction and learning the craft of storytelling. He worked as a designer and producer in the video games industry for a number of years as well as working in technology and admin services. He enjoys writing both serious and comedic science fiction and fantasy. Chris lives with his wife and an ever-growing population of critters.

CRIMSON MYTH PRESS

Crimson Myth Press offers more books by this author as well as books from a few other hand-picked authors. From science fiction & fantasy to adventure & mystery, we bring the best stories for adults and kids alike.

Check out our complete book catalog:

www.CrimsonMyth.com

Printed in Great Britain
by Amazon